5.0 out of 5 stars <u>YUMMY! YUMMY! YUMMY</u> <u>next book from this author.</u>

Reviewed in the United States on June 25, 2015

Verified Purchase

Abby (Abigail) Simon is a very human delightful character—she's spunky and sometimes smart mouthed, kind, thoughtful, a loyal friend, a great cook and the owner of a business she established in the small town of Elk River Minnesota—a pastry shop called "Dessert First." She also has a wonderful relationship with her parents—but especially her father.

There is nothing shallow about Abby. She is resilient and strong, but she is still reeling from the devastation of having her groom-to-be (Adam Jackson) show up at her door a couple of hours before the wedding ceremony and tell her he couldn't go through with the wedding. A year later he has never told her why, even though he tried to keep in touch with her after that tragic day, phoning her regularly until she took a stand and told him not to call her again. Kudos to her! She decided to move on…but everyone she dated is a bust because in her heart she still had feelings for him.

Then Max James comes back to town and moves back into his parents' house next door to her mom and dad. His mother has had a stroke and he has moved home to help them deal with what has happened. Through her teens, Abby had lived with a heart-wrenching crush on this neighbor boy who never even seen her as anything more than the kid from next door. When he left at the age of 18, to go to the University of Texan and study to become an architect, he hadn't given her a second glance. Now, thirteen years later, he is stunned when he sees her—the scrawny tom-boy that he had known had a crush on him then, as turned into real beauty—and it is Max's turn to be smitten. But Abby is guarded—she hasn't forgotten the mean things he and his friends did to her for laughs a way back then. She's older and wiser now, and while he is too handsome for his own good, and he still makes her heart do crazy things, she's not falling at his feet. He sets out to build a relationship with her.

And then just when things look promising, Adam Jackson insists that he has to talk to Abby and tell her why he called off the wedding. He insists that he has regretted his decision, and he wants to make a second chance.

I was already smitten by Max, and I wanted her to tell Adam it was too little too late, but Abby still had questions in her heart. And so, she decided to reconsider, and I almost prayed that she would choose Max, but the heart has its own ways.

Connie Stephany has created characters that I could relate too, and the whole book is woven into their everyday lives, and those of the secondary characters are a realistic part of the whole. I love romances that have more depth than "the girl gets the boy, the boy gets the girl" thing from the past and this author has done that in this book.

I bought this book because the title "Second Chance" caught my eye. The theme of a second chance has been running through my mind, and my own work, and I wanted to see what this new author had written. I was not disappointed in the story.

Other reviewers have noted—as do I—that the book could be improved overall with some editing, tightening up in the sentence structure and cutting out unnecessary wording, and at first I had thought to give this book four stars because of that. However when the overall read is satisfying, I think that most readers who have not been involved in the editing process do not even notice these things that pop out at those who do edit…and my heart said 4.5 and I rounded it up to 5 stars because aside from those things that I noticed with a critical eye, I really did enjoy the book.

Congratulation Connie Stephany—I am looking forward to your next book!

5.0 out of 5 stars <u>TORN BETWEEN TWO LOVERS</u>

Reviewed in the United States on August 24, 2015

Verified Purchase

Since becoming a Book Reviewer about a year I can't help but notice the number of books I've read/review which has caused me to reminisce the years of my youth. Such is the case as I read this book by Connie Stephany.

This time it's a song called The Second Time Around in the 1960's sung by none other than Frank Sinatra; and if you read the lyrics to this sung, you'll see why I made the connection.

Love is lovelier the second time around
Just as wonderful with both feet on the ground
It's that second time you hear your love song sung
Makes you think perhaps that love, like youth, is wasted on the young
Love's more comfortable the second time you fall
Like a friendly home the second time you call
Who can say what brought us to this miracle we've found?
There are those who'll bet love comes but once, and yet
I'm oh, so glad we met the second time around.

While Abby had her first infatuation on a guy named Max thirteen years ago, but the problem is it had only been one way. But with his sudden return, it is now both ways.

As for Adam, the devoted guy she had been slated to marry, he disappeared leaving Abby alone at the altar. Now, just as her relationship with Max is taking off, he decides to return and to once again ask Abby to marry him. And just like the words of the song by Mary MacGregor [Peter, Paul, and Mary], she's torn between these lovers, feeling like a fool and knows that loving both of them would be breaking all the rules.

If you've ever had been in this same situation, having to choose between two guys who you love, then you can relate to one of the toughest decisions Abby will ever have to make in her life.

Ms. Stephany's writing is one which allows you to experience what the main characters in the book are, which is why I'm giving it 5 STARS.

5.0 out of 5 stars Highly recommend! Great read.

Reviewed in the United States on July 30, 2015

Verified Purchase

This is a very sweet romance where a successful owner is forced to choose between two men from her past.

It's a very sweet story, has many well-written flashbacks to help with character development and highlights the importance of friendship.

I recommend this romance novel!!!

5.0 out of 5 stars Precious characters & story

Reviewed in the United States on February 2, 2015

Verified Purchase

After reading this precious story I found I am not as forgiving as I thought I was. I was soooooo hoping Abby would not take Adam back as her boyfriend. I was truly rooting for Max to marry Abby. This was a charming, true to life story. Seeing that Ms. Stephany's next book is Adam & Jennifer's story it will be interesting to see if my opinion changes. Can't wait to read it!

5.0 out of 5 stars A superbly sumptuous read - sample this book now!

Reviewed in the United States on April 17, 2015

This is a sumptuous book. On the surface it appears to be a wholesome, heart-warming romance, but in fact it's a dissection of relationships and what motivates people to do what they do. Weaved amongst the pages, there are characters who enjoy subjugating others for pleasure - using their weakness to dominate and deceive. And in balance, there are other characters who show compassion, genuine care and interest for another's life and wellbeing. These secondary characters create a maze of emotions for the main characters to navigate through. Connie's gentle but captivating writing style takes you on that journey and you live those experiences, the hurt, the joy and of course, the hope of there being a chance to find love again. The central character Abby is a truly delightful woman who is jilted at her wedding by her fiancé Adam. Throughout the book, the reader, like Abby is waiting for the reason why. This immediately invests the reader to feel Abby's pain but also delivers a heightened sense of intrigue. What would really make someone say they can't marry their beloved on their big day? As a writer myself, all kinds of scenarios manifested in my mind, and this only drew me further into the story. It must be said, I'm not a chick lit kind of girl, and my usual diet is that of hard core thrillers that hold nothing back, however Second Chances enthralled me and I loved reading it. I can't pretend that at times I wanted Abby to explode and give certain characters a good thrashing or at least a vicious whipping with her tongue! Although, I understand that it wouldn't have been in her character at all, it would however have delivered just 'Desserts' to people who mistreated her. Abby as a woman, has a bit of 'super' attached to her; she makes great desserts from the crack of dawn, is a successful business woman, looks ravishingly edible herself (even with no make up!), spends time with elderly friends, organises her best friend's party & wedding and is a great track driver (with virtually no training!). Is it any wonder men are fighting over her? And yet, all of this doesn't come over as heavy or unbelievable. It all seems natural, and therein lies the skill of Connie's writing. The character of Max, I didn't warm to at first, as I was seeing him through a lens Connie wanted me to see through. An interesting device which kept me hooked, and I was pleased to be enlightened to his real disposition when that moment came. The focus on desserts and cakes is a fascinating aside, and enables the storyline to be seamlessly strung through, giving rise to long, lingering looks over the ice cream cakes. Such scenes also made me feel quite hungry whilst reading! Overall, Second Chances is a superb read by a talented author with much more to entice and attract than your average cupcake chick lit. Highly recommended.

5.0 out of 5 stars A Must Read!

Reviewed in the United States on June 13, 2016

What a charming novel! It was sweet and held more depth than I realized. The writing was superb, and there wasn't a point in the whole story that slowed down unnecessary.

We meet the main character, Abby, who is a loving, generous woman madly in love with the man she is about to marry, Adam. When he leaves her without warning, Abby is completely devastated not to mention confused. We journey with her as she puts her life back together, and takes a leap of faith in an old schoolmate by the name of Max. Just as things begin to get exciting for the two of them, Adam returns and Abby is torn between forgiveness and new love.

I know the storyline sounds cliché but bear with it, really. This is a story that pulls at your heartstrings, and makes you laugh. From the flashbacks to the present in time moments, you'll find yourself falling in love with these characters and at the end; you yourself won't be able to choose. Should Abby stay with Adam? Or move on with Max?

A must read for any romance novel fan.

Second Chances

CONNIE STEPHANY

ISBN: 979-8-89031-634-9 (sc)
ISBN: 979-8-89031-635-6 (hc)
ISBN: 979-8-89031-636-3 (e)

Because of the dynamic nature of the Internet, any web addresses or links contained in this book may have changed since publication and may no longer be valid. The views expressed in this work are solely those of the author and do not necessarily reflect the views of the publisher, and the publisher hereby disclaims any responsibility for them.

THE EWINGS
PUBLISHING

One Galleria Blvd., Suite 1900, Metairie, LA 70001
(504) 702-6708

Acknowledgments

First, I want to say thank you to my sister, Cari Peterson, for reading my book several times, and then helping me to edit it over a long weekend. You helped make my book something I can be truly proud of!

Second, I want to thank Sam Wicks, my favorite sister-in-law, for helping me to design the book cover. I love it!

Next, I want to thank my children who continued to spread the word that their mom is going to be a famous author. Even if that doesn't happen, I will be famous to them!

Lastly, I want to thank my amazing husband, Bob, who always encouraged me to realize my dream and convinced me to finally get it published.

Contents

Chapter 1

An Anniversary to Forget

Abigail Simon had the worst headache of her life.

She shook her head and cursed her best friend, "Damn you, Colleen." It made Abby's head pound harder.

"What's that, dear?"

Abby wasn't entirely sure if the voice belonged to her employee, Madeline, or if it was a customer. She was hoping it was Madeline.

"Never mind," Abby grumbled, rubbing her face.

Colleen always said when you need a break from reality, nothing worked better than a girl's night out (heavy drinking assumed).

Abby had to admit it was totally worth the headache, but the reality break was only temporary. The second Abby opened her eyes that morning, reality came back to smack her right in the face. A whole year later and Abby still hadn't figured out why Adam Jackson had left her on their wedding day.

She knew the memories would always remain, but for that one day, Abby had planned on sitting at home feeling sorry for herself, drinking a bottle of wine and watching chick flicks all night.

She thought her plan was the perfect way to mark the occasion. Her best friend hadn't agreed.

As Abby's head started to pound harder, her thoughts drifted to the night before. If she wanted to be fair, she would admit the headache was really courtesy of the two lemon drops, a shot of tequila, a duck fart, and a B52. However, it made Abby feel better to blame someone, so she was blaming Colleen.

"Madeline, do you have any Ibuprofen?" Abby asked her loyal friend as she walked by. "The stuff I took this morning wore off and I forgot to bring some with me."

"You betcha. I'll get it for ya right away," Madeline replied in her deep Minnesotan accent and walked away to get it.

What a good friend Madeline was. Too bad Abby wasn't thinking that way about Colleen that way right that moment.

Instead of just letting Abby sit at home alone, her best friend convinced her to go out on the town. Abby supposed she should really thank Colleen, considering proof of a great time was a massive hangover and a fuzzy memory of the night's events, but she wasn't feeling that generous.

What made everything worse was that she didn't even get to sleep that morning. As the owner of a local pastry shop in Elk River, Minnesota, named "Dessert First", Abby almost always made it in on Sunday mornings, her busiest day of the week. Although she didn't roll in until 7:30 am, she was still proud of herself that she had made it in at all.

As Madeline brought Abby the two Ibuprofen and a large glass of cold water, she thanked the heavens above for being the best employee in the world. Madeline had promised to come in and cover for Abby in the morning. She had told Abby she could cover for her the whole day, but Abby's favorite day was Sunday.

Abby glanced over at the clock hanging on the blue and white wall and sighed in relief. She wasn't sure how she'd done it, but she managed to make it through the day and it was just about time to close up shop.

Abby smiled despite her headache, thinking of her shop. It was her pride and joy. She loved making desserts and breakfast rolls and just about anything sweet and loved serving them to her customers. It gave her deep satisfaction to see the look on their faces when they tried something they loved, something *she* created.

She even had customers tell her they loved her after trying her delicious treats, but unfortunately, most of them had been women, and the ones that had been men were usually sitting next to their elderly wives.

"I know you were here early, but can you close up shop today, Madeline?" Abby asked, who she thought of more as a second mother or a good friend than her employee.

"Oh yeah, ya know I will. I told ya not to even come in today!" She reminded Abby. "Are ya going to your parents tonight, dear?" Madeline asked.

"Yes. My parents are expecting me in a little while," Abby replied.

"You go on and get ready then. I'll close everything up for the night," Madeline told her and tried to shoo her away. Abby stubbornly just stood there waiting for the doors to close for the day, a habit that was hard to break even with her loyal employee telling her to get lost.

As Madeline tried to get Abby moving, she found herself wondering why Abby had such trouble with men. Abby was a very pretty woman; she was curvy in all the right places and Madeline figured it was the type of body many women her age longed to have. Abby's long, blonde hair was slightly wavy and Madeline had overheard more than one compliment from both men and women alike. Madeline finally gave up trying to get Abby moving and walked towards the door to close up the shop.

Abby watched Madeline walk to the front of the store and turn the sign from "Open" to "Please Come Again" and then lock the door.

Only then did Abby finally make her way to the back of the shop, grabbing her backpack on the way.

When she got to the small office in the back, she looked at herself in the full-length mirror hanging on the door and groaned very loudly.

"Shoot!" Abby muttered to herself. She couldn't go to her parent's house looking like *that*. Her mother would never let her hear the end of it.

Abby closed her eyes to shield them from the sight of her pale face, and the moment they were closed the picture of her fiancé showing up at her door the morning of their wedding flashed into her head.

Although alcohol, a few bummed smokes, and dancing all night to the eighties band playing at the local bar in town were very successful in stifling the memories of the night before, it, unfortunately, seemed to be doing the exact opposite to her that day.

In her mind, she could see herself opening her front door, and thinking it was odd Adam had shown up hours before the wedding after they had agreed not to see each other. But even at that point, she still hadn't known she wouldn't be getting married that day.

Abby's eyes snapped back open. No! She was not going to think about this right now!

While she slapped on a fresh coat of makeup and toyed with her hair, Abby's mind wandered, thinking of anything and everything as long as it had nothing to do with Adam. The to-do list in her mind was always there and always had several things for Abby to remember.

She needed toilet paper, ink cartridges, garlic powder, toothpaste, and coffee creamer. She also planned to buy Sophie Kinsella's new book and she needed to get a gift for her cousin's baby shower. She needed to remember to water the new flowers she had planted and she had to remember to run to the bank on Monday. Had she remembered to grab the mail yesterday?

Abby also wanted to remember to pack up a dessert to bring over to her parents' neighbor, George James, who was home alone waiting for his wife, Junie, to recover from her recent stroke. Abby's desserts always made George happy and she figured he could use a little cheering up. They were such a nice couple and they were always happy to see her.

Abby looked at herself in the mirror and decided she looked as good as she was going to get after a night like she had. She went back up to the front of the store and placed two grasshopper bars, one of George's favorites, into a small to-go box.

She grabbed her stuff, and said, "Madeline, I'm leaving now. I'll see you Tuesday." Her shop was closed on Mondays and she was looking forward to the day off so she could fully recover.

"Bye, honey. Say hello to your parents," Madeline replied. "And take care of yourself!"

"Will do," Abby replied.

Abby walked out the back door and jumped in her car, looking back at her shop before pulling away and driving down the street.

Abby had opened her shop with a ton of hard work and very long days and it was successful in less than a year after opening.

Even before finding Madeline, when she was so busy, she had very little time for herself, she never once regretted opening "Dessert First". She didn't even regret it on those cold Minnesota winter mornings when it was 20 below zero with 30 below zero wind chill and she'd have to get up and be at the shop to start baking by 4:00 am. She loved it.

Abby had met so many interesting people at her bakery. There had been plenty of good-looking men who came into her shop and a few had asked her out, but up to that point, she never had time to even contemplate dates.

That changed when Adam Jackson walked into her pastry shop for the first time. Adam had told Abby later his family had raved to him about Abby's special caramel rolls and freshly brewed coffee so he came in to try them for himself.

Abby didn't know how it happened but Adam had found his way back into her thoughts. Damn him. This time she let her mind take her to the first time she saw Adam, and her heart broke a little more just thinking about that happy memory.

Three years earlier...

It was a beautiful fall Sunday, and Abby was working the front of the store, serving coffee refills to her favorite customers with a large smile on her face. Sunday was her favorite day at the shop, with families coming in to spend time together and try her goodies.

As she turned back to the front of the store to make more coffee, Abby looked up to see one of the hottest guys she'd ever seen walking into her shop with an older couple and a younger woman. She stopped dead in her tracks and almost dropped the coffee pot. She snapped out of it before he caught her staring.

When Abby made it to their table, the gorgeous man looked up at her and gave her a huge smile.

"Hi there," The man said to Abby in a low, rumbly voice.

Abby looked at him for a few seconds too long and then mentally slapped herself. She swallowed and put a giant smile on her face.

"Hi, everyone. How are you today? Anyone care for some coffee?" She was proud of herself for not stuttering the greeting out and instead sounding confident, something she didn't feel at all after staring.

The man was way too handsome for his own good with an incredible body to go along with it. He had light blonde hair and chocolate brown eyes, which seemed like a rare combination to Abby.

As she waited for their responses to her offer of coffee, she wondered if the young woman sitting at the table was his girlfriend or sister or just a friend. After a glance, she noticed there was no ring on either of their fingers, but that didn't necessarily mean anything.

"Yes, we'd all like some coffee, please." The man answered, looking right into Abby's eyes.

Abby stared right back at him and was proud of herself for smiling and then looking away first.

Abby started to fill everyone's cups at the table, and after Mr. Hottie went back to reviewing his menu, Abby took her opportunity and quickly checked him out. His arm muscles were bulging in his white T-shirt, his pecs were perfectly sized and he had a flat stomach. She could only imagine the six-pack underneath.

The. Man. Was. Hot.

"Do you need a few minutes to look over the menu?" Abby asked, praying they'd say yes.

She needed a few minutes to get her pulse under control. She was glancing down at the young woman, again wondering about the relationship. In looking at her more closely, she's sort of looked like the older couple and had the same color hair as the hot one, with the same eyes.

"No, I think we're all set. We all came for your special caramel rolls." The older lady answered for the table.

"Okay, Mom, I guess we're all having caramel rolls," Adam said with a grin at Abby.

"Those are my specialty. You won't be disappointed, I assure you! Four caramel rolls coming right up," Abby answered and walked off to get the rolls for them before her heart exploded.

A few minutes later, after her pulse slowed to an almost normal pace, she walked back to the table with the four warm, gooey caramel rolls and set one in front of each of the four people sitting at the table. She had also brought the coffee pot and refilled their empty cups.

"Enjoy!" Abby said and walked away.

The rest of the time he was in her shop, she pretended he wasn't one of the hottest guys she'd ever met and served him like anyone else, except maybe she gave him an extra glance or two. To her utter embarrassment, he caught her eye once and shot her a wink.

Abby went back to the table a short while later to check on them.

"Well?" She asked the table. "What did you think of the caramel rolls?"

"Delicious. You were right. We were not disappointed." The young woman answered, smiling at Abby. "My brother even finished what I couldn't."

Brother. Yes!

Abby gave the woman a huge grin.

"Great! Please come back soon and try our other treats. All freshly baked and my own recipes!" She told them all, glancing at the man last and smiling.

"I will," He replied back at her with a grin.

When the man left that morning, Abby was sad to see him go but was pleasantly surprised to see him walk in the front door the following day.

He bought a dozen of her secret recipe brown butter chocolate chip cookies and talked to Abby for several minutes. He also introduced himself. Adam was a very fitting name for him, Abby thought to herself.

After thanking her for the cookies, Abby sighed as she watched him walk towards the door to leave. Her eyes naturally lowered and settled on his rock-hard behind. His designer jeans fit him perfectly.

7

He stopped in his tracks, whipped around, and came back up to the counter. She barely had time to move her eyes back up to his face before he caught her staring at his butt.

"Did you forget something?" Abby asked Adam with a smile, looking into his delicious brown eyes. She knew she was blushing as she was wondering if he had caught her staring at his perfect behind.

"Yes. I was wondering if you would be interested in going out to dinner with me." Adam asked Abby, a grin on his face.

"Yes, I'd like that."

Adam's smile had lit up his entire face and Abby almost lost it.

"Great! How about Saturday night?" Adam asked her.

"That works for me," Abby replied, returning the smile. She reached under the counter and grabbed one of her business cards, writing her cell phone number on the back, and then handing it to him.

"Perfect. I'll give you a call later this week." Adam said as he reached out to take the card from her.

"Sounds good." She was proud of herself for speaking clearly and not falling back to her stuttering phase from years past.

"I better let you get back to work. Have a great day! I'll call you later," He repeated and then turned around to leave. As he walked out the door, he turned back around to give a little wave and Abby waved back, this time careful to keep her eyes at face-level until he turned back around to walk out the door.

♥ ♥ ♥

It was a good memory, but it just made her feel sad all over again and made her think of that awful day when her life fell apart and her heart was broken into a million pieces.

She did not want to think about that day before going in to see her parents. She didn't want her mom to have any more of a reason to give her the third degree, even though she knew it would come anyway.

Abby finally pulled up in the driveway of her childhood home, hoping her mom and dad and dinner would be a diversion even if for a little while. She started walking quickly up the sidewalk because she was late. Thinking she had to bring George's dessert over to him after dinner, she glanced over at their house and almost tripped over her own feet.

Right before her eyes stood a man whose hotness factor was the highest rating possible, easily hot enough to rival Adam's.

He had very dark hair, so dark it was almost black, and the perfect body, with large, manly shoulders that tapered down to his tight abs. Since he was wearing a tank top, she could see his perfectly sculpted arms straining as he hauled boxes into the house and she almost swallowed her tongue.

An intense feeling of Déjà vu washed over her. Although it had been thirteen long years, she recognized him instantly.

Chapter 2

A Blast from the Past

Max James walked out of his father's house and up to the moving van, wondering what he'd grab next. He brought everything he owned with him since he planned to just stay in Minnesota and eventually move into his own home.

He planned to help his parents for a while and then start looking for some land close to them. He planned to design and help build a home for himself. In the meantime, he would store everything in his parent's huge unfinished basement.

Max grabbed a box holding dishes from the moving van, walked carefully down the stairs, and then started walking toward the front door. He noticed something move out of the corner of his eye and glanced over to the house next door.

He just about dropped the box of dishes he was holding due to utter shock. He stopped in his tracks, mouth wide open, and gaped at the prettiest damn woman he'd ever seen. She had a body a man lusted after, had long, wavy blond hair, and looked like she walked right off of the cover of a magazine. Could that be his old neighbor, Abby, the girl who used to stare at him and stutter every time she talked to him?

♥ ♥ ♥

Abby recovered and continued walking towards the front porch of her parents' gray two-story house thinking this time around was different. Although she had a momentary lapse when she first saw him, she was no longer the silly kid with a crush.

She picked up the pace a little, while thinking she had narrowly escaped being noticed. She hadn't thought of Max in a long time, especially since it had been so many years since she'd last seen him. She was almost up to her parents' front porch when Abby heard him call her name.

Max was standing there, holding the box of dishes as he tried to find his voice. "Abby?" Max called to her.

She contemplated ignoring him, pretending she didn't hear him but then she heard her name again. Damn!

"Hey, Abby!" Max called a little louder, still holding the box of dishes.

Abby turned her head, smiled, and answered with a little wave. And then she kept walking toward her parents' front porch. She may have been over the man, but that certainly didn't mean she'd want him to see her looking so horrible from the previous night's partying.

Max put down the box he was carrying and started heading across the lawn separating the two homes. He hadn't seen Abby for many years and was almost embarrassed to admit he had sort of forgotten about her.

He certainly didn't expect to see her all grown up. Seeing her brought back memories of a tall, awkward kid. Now she was this amazingly beautiful woman, and he was instantly attracted to her.

"Abby, how are you?" Max asked her, standing only a few feet away.

Abby whipped around at the sound of his voice, surprised to see him so close. How did he get there so fast? She hadn't even realized he had been walking towards her. She was even more surprised he remembered her name.

"I'm great, Max. How are you?" Abby answered, continuing to walk up the steps of her parents' front porch.

She was proud that she was able to utter the words clearly because he was even more handsome than she remembered and she was starting to think impure thoughts. Damn, was she starting to blush?

"I'm good," Max said and then continued after her. "Hey, wait. Are you in a hurry?" Max asked, chuckling and wondering why she seemed so eager to get inside. She was pretty from far away, but up close she was stunning. He wanted to talk to her for the first time in his life, although it sure didn't seem like she wanted to talk to him.

Hearing his low chuckle, Abby let out a sigh and turned back to Max. He gave her a knee-weakening grin and she looked into the bluest eyes she'd ever seen. His body was even better up close. It was hard not to notice with his tight white tank hugging every muscle. Go figure he'd get to see her looking her worst.

She gave him a small smile.

She wanted to answer yes, that she was most definitely in a hurry because she couldn't wait to get away from him. What a complete chicken.

Instead, Abby shook her head and said, "Well, no, I guess not." She turned more toward him, leaned against her parent's front porch, and asked, "What are you doing here?"

Abby knew her question was fully loaded, asking both what he was doing moving into his parent's house after 13 years and partly what he was doing over here at her parents' house talking to her when he had never done it before in their lives.

Max raised his eyebrow at her and answered her question. "I moved back to help take care of my mom and dad while my mom is recovering. They're getting older and with my mom's stroke a couple of weeks ago and my dad's bad leg, they need my help for a while. My mom comes home from the hospital soon. They wouldn't hear of moving into a home, but they did agree to let me move in to help."

Abby's heart melted a little. "I was so sorry to hear about your mom's stroke. I hope she's doing better," Abby replied sincerely.

She wasn't sure if he had any idea how often she visited his parents, but really doubted it. Although she no longer had her silly school-girl crush, she still cared for his parents because they had always treated her well.

She loved to bring them her latest creations; they were always up to trying a new dessert and gave their honest opinions, although she could only remember one time, they didn't like her dessert. It was a horrible recipe she'd found in an old cookbook of her mothers and the main ingredient was marmalade. She shuttered just thinking about it.

Max said, "Yes, she's doing much better now and my dad is very eager to have her home."

Before she could say anything, Max switched topics quickly, wanting to know more about Abby. "So, what's new with you? Career? Married? Kids?" Smooth, Max, real smooth, he told himself.

He shot her another grin.

Abby pulled herself together and smiled back at Max, answering his question with very little detail. "Not married and no kids." She looked down at the to-go box in her hand. "I own a pastry shop in town. Hey, since you're headed that way, do you want to give this to your dad? I was going to drop it over there after dinner but maybe you can bring it back for him and just tell him I'll see him soon?"

"Sure, I can give it to him. I hadn't heard about your shop, but now that I have, I'll definitely come and try it out," Max told her and he reached out and took the box from her.

His fingers accidentally skimmed hers and Abby nearly dropped the box when she felt the jolt of electricity run through her body. Abby quickly pulled her hand away and looked down. What the hell was that?

"Your dad can show you where it is," She told him, trying to recover and doing her best to ignore her tingling hand from where his hand had skimmed hers. Get your crap together, Abby!

She didn't ask about his dating status, although she wondered what he'd been doing since his divorce. Abby remembered clearly when Max had gotten married, and it had stung when she had heard the news. Later, Max's dad told her when his marriage ended after only two years.

"Well, I guess I can let you go inside, but we should get together for a cup of coffee or dinner and catch up." He looked at her hopefully. He just couldn't get over how much she'd changed in those thirteen years. How in the hell was she not taken?

Abby raised her eyebrow. "Yes, we'll have to, ah, catch up sometime." She looked down at her feet to hide her smile.

13

Catch up? She wondered what they'd talk about that they hadn't just covered in the last two minutes. They probably spoke more today than they ever had growing up.

She kept her thoughts to herself, glad that she occasionally knew when to use her filter to keep her mouth shut. She forced the smile from her face and looked back up at him. "I better get inside now; my parents are expecting me. Nice to see you again, Max. Tell your dad I'll talk to him soon and please tell your mom hello," Abby said.

She didn't wait for a reply. She turned on her heel and walked inside. She shut the door and then leaned back against it, letting out a long, slow breath. There was one thing for certain; that man hadn't lost his appeal.

Abby closed her eyes, thinking about him for another second while she caught her breath.

Max's tan made his blue eyes clear and bright, the color of the ocean in Mexico, and his body was good enough to be on the cover of a calendar. She was over her school-girl crush, she told herself harshly, but what the hell was with the spark that tore through her body when he accidentally touched her?

Memories came flooding back, remembering another time when she felt that spark.

Fourteen years earlier...

Abby was almost a mile away from her house, and all of a sudden, her bike chain broke. She was almost in tears as she tried to get the chain back on her bike.

It was embarrassing at 14 years of age to have a bike as her only method of transportation and then to have it break was mortifying.

Max just happened to be driving by, thankfully by himself. He had noticed Abby stranded, trying to put the chain on her bike herself and he pulled over to the side of the road.

"Did your chain break, Abby?" Max asked her, even though he could clearly see the problem.

Abby just nodded shyly.

Max took out the toolbox from his car, which he always had with him.

"Can you hold up your bike, Abby, while I put the chain back on?" Max asked her, while he was leaning over, looking at the bike chain.

"Sure," Abby replied, barely even a whisper.

They spent a few minutes in silence, while Max adeptly put the bike chain back in its rightful place.

"There, you go. All fixed!" Max said proudly.

"Thanks," Abby replied timidly, still standing there, looking at Max.

"Glad to help," He replied. Max just stared at Abby, with a proud grin on his face. She was still just a kid, but she was starting to grow up a little. He thought she'd maybe someday be a real looker.

Abby finally grabbed the handles and she accidentally touched Max's hand. Her hand jerked back as if she'd been burned, and was really embarrassed by her reaction.

"Thanks, again," Abby said quietly, and then took off towards her house.

♥ ♥ ♥

Max was left standing outside on Abby's front porch.

Was he crazy or was she extremely eager to get inside, away from him? Had he been mean to her growing up? He knew she'd had a little crush on him, but how did he treat her?

Thinking back, he remembered mostly just ignoring her. She'd stare at him and stutter every time she'd try to talk to him. His friends would tease her, but he told them to leave her alone so they stopped.

The crush wasn't wanted when he was 18 and she was 15. Thirteen years later, it was a different story. Max found himself wishing for the looks she used to give him.

Max finally headed back over to his parents' house to get back to unloading the boxes from the moving truck. He was trying to figure out when he'd see her again so he could ask her out on a date.

As he walked up to his parents' house, he saw a young girl ride by on a bike. He suddenly had a flashback of the time he found Abby on the side of the road with a broken bike chain. He had been 17 years old at that time and remembered it clearly because he had just found out that day he had gotten into the University of Texas. He already knew he wanted to study Architecture.

He remembered feeling sorry for her, seeing her on the side of the road. She must have been shy because she barely said two words to him, uttering a quiet "Thank You" when he finished putting the chain back on her bike. Then, she just rode away.

He remembered thinking she had really grown up in the five years he'd known her. It wasn't like he'd miss her, but she was finally starting to look a little more like a girl than a little tomboy.

♥ ♥ ♥

As Abby sat there against her parent's front door, still trying to catch her breath, she thought about the past. She had a full-blown crush on Max by the time she was 13 years old. He was three years older than her, and the crush was very obvious. Unfortunately for her, she was a late bloomer and still looked like a little girl at that age. A lot of her friends, including her best friend Colleen, had started getting their breasts much earlier and were wearing bras but she was stick-thin and still had no sign of them.

Her mind took her back even further, to the first time she met Max.

♥ ♥ ♥

Eighteen years earlier...

It was Labor Day weekend, right before the start of 5th grade when she was outside practicing basketball at her house.

The summer sun was warm and made her sweat harder as she played basketball, completely soaking her hair within ten minutes.

As she was dribbling the ball on the driveway, she noticed a man and a woman moving into the house next door taking boxes out of the truck and bringing them inside. She had just started wondering if they had any kids when out of the house walked a young boy who wore his dark hair a little too long, which allowed it to curl over his ears a little. He was wearing a dark green tank top and jean shorts and he was very tan from the summer sun.

Being only 10, she didn't know how to hide her fascination. She was pretty sure he was the cutest boy she'd ever seen, the only possible exception being Jordan Knight from New Kids on the Block, who just so happened to be on a poster hanging on her bedroom wall. She dropped the ball and just stared at him. The bouncing ball caught his eye, which then stopped in the grass between their homes. He looked up to find where the ball had come from, noticed her watching him and he gave her a little wave. She screamed loudly, covered her face, and ran inside her house.

♥ ♥ ♥

Abby had forgotten about that and laughed at herself, trying to keep quiet so her parents wouldn't hear. Remembering her reaction made Abby blush in embarrassment even eighteen years later.

It wasn't exactly all roses having a crush on Max James, either. She was pretty sure he knew about her crush and Max's friends took advantage of it.

It was amazing to her that she hadn't figured out they were just using her and teasing her every chance they got. She was so completely naïve back then.

Max's friends would send her on errands to the store down the street or they would have her pick up the mess they left outside.

They'd sometimes convince her to do some of Max's chores so he could leave with them. Abby was more than happy to do whatever they wanted to get Max to notice her.

They often told her if she kept it up, she'd soon be Max's girlfriend and she loved the idea so much she didn't even think of the possibility that they were lying. Max didn't pay much attention to her, but that was probably just as painful as being teased by his friends. He wouldn't even look at her when she was around, even though she did everything she could think of to get him to notice her.

The first time he truly hurt her was when his friends told her Max wanted to take her out on a date when she was almost fifteen.

Fourteen years earlier...

"Be ready by 7:00 pm, okay? Max will pick you up at your house so you can just wait on your front porch." Pete had told her, smiling at her.

She looked at Pete and skeptically asked, "Why didn't Max just ask me?"

Pete looked confident and said, "Max is just too shy and worried you'd say no."

Abby wanted it to be true so badly that she went with his explanation and said, "Okay, I'll be ready."

"Cool. He'll be excited. I'll tell him," Pete told her and walked away.

Abby was so excited. She found a really cute dress to wear, one that still had the tags on because a dress wasn't something she wore often. She fixed her hair and worked extra hard on her makeup, which her mom had just started letting her wear. She spun around in front of her mirror, thinking how lucky she was to finally be going out with her crush of so many years. She had told her mom that she was going to a movie with a friend but hadn't mentioned it was Max. Abby was ready by 6:45 pm, but she made herself wait to go out on her front porch until 7:00 pm so that she didn't seem too eager.

She got excited as she saw Max walk out the front door and turn towards Abby's house, giving her a little wave.

Then, he walked towards his car and hopped in. She could almost remember the sound of his car roaring to life because it had been in dire need of a muffler. She watched him back out of his driveway, getting even more excited. He was really coming!

The excitement lasted three seconds but then swiftly turned to confusion as she watched Max drive away in the opposite direction of her house. She hadn't noticed that his friends were already in his convertible when he got in so she was treated to further embarrassment as Max drove away and his friends turned around and looked at her, laughing, pointing, and giving each other high-fives.

When it finally clicked in her mind what had happened, she ran inside, right up to her room, and cried. Abby remembered her mom had come to her room, asking her what was wrong, and why didn't go to the movie. She told her mom she didn't feel well and didn't come out of her room until the next morning. She just couldn't believe Max would do that and would let his friends do that to her.

Abby had eventually forgiven him for that cruel joke because she wasn't entirely sure if he was in on it or if it was just his friends.

Abby really wished she had just given up on her crush at that point, but she hadn't. It could have saved her the heartbreak she felt the summer he left for college.

Thirteen years earlier...

Abby was playing basketball outside, ironically just like she'd been doing the first time she saw Max, and noticed a moving truck had pulled up to his house. Max and his friends had begun packing boxes into the truck. Like the day she first laid eyes on him, she stopped and stared, this time watching them load everything into the moving truck. Eventually, one of his friends noticed her staring and wandered over to her driveway.

Pete eagerly told her the news to watch her face. "Did you hear? Max is going away to college."

Abby swallowed hard, and asked softly, "Oh?"

Pete just gave her a big smile and said, "Yeah, he's going to the University of Texas. That's like a million miles away from here."

Abby just shrugged and tried to hide the fact that she was devastated. She knew he would be going to college in the fall but she had hoped he'd go to the University of Minnesota.

"That's cool," She answered and tried really hard to fight it but her eyes welled up.

Pete started laughing. "Are you crying?" he asked incredulously, pointing at her face.

"Of course not!" She managed to spit out at him, but she was so embarrassed she ran inside and up to her room.

She could remember feeling like her life was over. She cried for what must have been almost an hour and by the time she looked out her window, the moving truck was gone and Max's car was no longer in the driveway.

♥ ♥ ♥

Abby had to admit it was fun to see Max, years later, even though she wasn't looking her best. It was fun to go down memory lane. She never ran into him when he visited, and Abby thought his recent pictures didn't do him justice.

Abby shook her head to clear Max from her mind, pushing herself away from the door and walking toward the kitchen, figuring her parents were wondering where she was. "Mom? Dad?

Where are you?" She called out.

Abby heard her mom from the kitchen. "We're in here, honey."

Abby walked into the kitchen, thinking it defined her mom. A couple of years ago her parents had updated the kitchen. It had been her mother's favorite place in the house before they remodeled, but now they couldn't get her out of it. The countertops were updated with black granite which contrasted nicely with the stainless steel, best-in-class appliances. They replaced the old linoleum floor with hardwood cherry floors and matching cupboards. The final touch was the coffee bar décor with paintings on the wall, rugs on the floor, and matching towels. It was the perfect place to have a hot cup of coffee on a Sunday morning.

"Hey Mom, you'll never guess who I just ran into," Abby said.

"Oh? Who is that, dear?" Asked her mom, looking up from the stove at Abby.

"Max James," Abby told her. "He's apparently moving in with his parents to help them out for a while," Abby told her. She turned towards her mom and asked "Did you know, mom?"

"Oh, I had heard about it." She waved the question away with her hand. "George told me that last week and I forgot to mention it." Abby's mom told her.

She quickly changed the subject. "How are you, honey? Are you doing ok? I tried calling you yesterday. What did you do all day?" Her mom bombarded her with questions, looking worried about her only daughter.

"Mom, I'm fine," Abby said to her. "I spent the day with Colleen." Abby paused, and then said quietly, "And then we went to the bar, got schnockered, and danced all night."

"I wish you'd have called. I worried about you all day!" Abby's mom scolded. And then as if she'd just realized what Abby said last, said to her, "Do you mean you got drunk?"

"I know, but I told you Mom, I just needed my best friend," Abby replied. Then shrugged her shoulders and said, "And yes, drunk. And I smoked three cigarettes," Abby added for good measure, holding up three fingers and giving her mom a smug look.

Abby heard footsteps and saw her dad walk into the kitchen. "Is that my little girl I hear?" He said and came up and gave Abby a huge hug. "How's my favorite daughter?" He asked.

"Your favorite daughter is just fine, Dad." She grinned at him. Abby was an only child.

"Did you hear her, Harold? She got drunk last night! And she smoked!" Her mom told him, exasperated.

Abby's dad looked at her mom. "Did she?" Then he looked back at Abby, grinned, and said, "Good for you!" So, what if she smoked when she drank? He had done the same thing when he was her age.

Her mom just shook her head and told them dinner was ready. They all headed into the dining room and sat down to eat.

As they ate dinner, Abby noticed her parents looking at each other, smiling.

"Okay, what gives?" Abby asked them. "Why do you guys keep looking at each other like you are hiding something and can't wait to tell me? Is everything okay?" She knew them very well and could tell something was up.

Her parents smiled at each other again, and then her dad pulled out an envelope. As he handed the envelope to Abby, he said, "Well, your mother and I saved up to send you on a little vacation."

"What?" Abby asked, wondering what he was talking about.

Her mother continued, "We wanted to send you on that trip you've always wanted to take but never took the time. We already cleared it with Madeline and some of your other staff to make sure they could cover while you're gone. You leave two days after Colleen's wedding!"

"What?" Abby asked again. "I don't understand. Where am I going?" She asked, getting a little excited, but thinking there was no way they'd know where to send her.

"You've talked forever about your dream vacation. You know exactly where we're sending you," Her dad told her.

"Are you serious? I'm going to Napa Valley?" Abby asked, still not sure where her parents were sending her. She wasn't sure they would know she'd always wanted to go on a trip to Napa, California, where she could explore the vineyards and try endless types of wine.

"Yes, ma'am!" Her mom said proudly.

"Oh my Gosh! I can't believe it!" Abby started thinking about exactly what she pictured as the dream vacation. She'd explore the vineyards, go out to a different restaurant for every meal, and at night she'd curl up with a good book and relax.

"Well, believe it honey. We want you to have a wonderful time. The trip is all set. You'll be staying at a little cottage in Sonoma, just fifteen minutes from Napa Valley. There are tons of tours you can take, and we've arranged a couple of them, like the one to the Robert Mondavi Winery, but most of it's up to you to figure out what you want to do. You'll have plenty of time for everything, Abby. You'll be there for 10 days."

"Really? Ten days!

I can't believe this. I never thought I'd get a chance to go. This is amazing. Thank you!" She said, getting more excited as she thought of exploring the wineries and eating delicious foods at some of the best restaurants in California.

For the rest of the meal, they talked about the different wineries her parents had found, in addition to the two tours they had already booked for her. After dinner, they went online to show her the little cottage she'd be staying in for those 10 glorious days. She had her own private little cottage that had a hot tub, a fireplace, and a beautiful backyard that had a gorgeous view of a vineyard in the distance.

A small part of Abby wished she'd be going with someone like Colleen, but part of her was happy to have the freedom to do exactly what she'd want to do the entire vacation.

She couldn't believe her parents had done that for her. She felt like the luckiest person in the world.

♥ ♥ ♥

Max went inside his parents' house and went in search of his dad. Maybe he'd know something about her.

"Dad? Dad! Where are you?" Max asked.

"I'm in the kitchen, Max. Come and eat something," Max's dad answered.

Max walked into the kitchen and looked around. The kitchen could use a little updating, he thought to himself. He knew his parents wouldn't do it though. His mom didn't cook much anymore and his dad never really did much other than to open up a can of soup when his mom wasn't there to cook for him.

"What are you eating, Dad?" Max asked.

He looked at his dad sitting at the table with a bowl of soup.

"Chicken noodle soup. Want some?"

Max's dad, George, replied and then noticed the white box Max was holding.

"Wait, what do you have there?" He recognized the white box from Abby's shop immediately.

"This is for you, from Abby," Max said, and he set it down in front of him. "Actually, I wanted to ask you about Abby," Max said.

23

George wasted no time opening the box and smiled when he saw what was inside. He decided he'd quickly eat his soup and then enjoy his favorite grasshopper bars. If Max was lucky, he may even share one since Abby was so nice and gave him two.

George looked up at Max. "Abby? I didn't even know you knew her name." His dad teased. "What do you want to know about her?" George asked, grinning, noticing the look of interest on his son's face. Hot damn! He was trying not to smile too hard. For some reason, he just knew once he saw her Max would be interested. She had turned into a real beauty while he was away. Everyone knew she had a crush on Max growing up, including George.

"Okay, Dad. I know, I know. Just tell me what you know. Have you been to her shop? Do you know if she's dating anyone?" He asked. He was almost embarrassed to ask his dad all of these questions, but he just had to find out.

"Of course, we've been to her place," George replied proudly, as if he had something to do with it, and then started to eat his soup again.

Max waited for an eternity and then asked, "Anything else you can tell me, Dad?"

It was painful for Max to wait while his dad just sat there and ate the rest of his soup.

When he was done, he brought his bowl to the sink, rinsed it out, put it in the dishwasher, and then came back and sat down. He placed one of the grasshopper bars on a napkin in front of himself, and then placed the other on another napkin and slid it across the table towards Max.

George took a bite of the bar, looked at Max, and then with a faraway look on his face, he finally said "Mom and I eat there all the time. Abby usually sits with us for a while. She always tells us she's trying out a new recipe and that we're her guinea pigs. Every dessert that girl makes is like a taste of heaven so we certainly don't mind trying them! Okay, except maybe one time. I think it had marmalade in it." He shuddered as looked at Max.

Then he smiled and continued, "She's been great to us over the years. Raking leaves, shoveling snow, and even grocery shopping for us once when we were both sick. She still brings us dinner once in a while."

George was sincere when he said all of this to Max. He'd like nothing better than to see him with a girl like Abby. He never really cared much for Rachel, Max's ex-wife, although he never told Max that. Rachel was too needy and materialistic and then to find out she had been cheating on him. He just didn't know what Max saw in her from the start. Abby was not either of those things, from what he'd seen over the years. He secretly had hoped Max would come home and see Abby and fall in love. In the last few years, whenever Max was home, Abby hadn't been around. Maybe it was finally his chance!

"Tell me what you think of her, Dad," Max laughed, shaking his head. "I didn't know she did all that for you. In fact, I don't know much about her at all. Maybe I'll stop into that place of hers." Max grinned. "Would you like to join me?" Max asked hopefully.

"I guess we could go there sometime." George replied, and then looked down at Max's dessert and said, "Are you going to eat your bar or not?"

"Hands off, Dad," Max replied, laughing, and then took a bite. "Hmm, this is good," He told his dad, and scarfed the whole bar down in a couple of bites, licking his fingers to remove the rest of the chocolate. "So, is she dating anyone? I can't imagine someone like her not dating anyone," Max said.

"That's something you'll have to find out on your own," George told him as he ate his grasshopper bar in little bites, savoring it.

He knew she wasn't dating anyone, but he'd have to find that out for himself. She had just been over the other day and they had chatted a little. He knew she was checking in on him while Junie was in the hospital, sweet thing. George hadn't told her Max was moving home, either. He wanted it to be a surprise for both of them.

"Well, I guess at least you know where her shop is so you can show me. I'll have to take that for now and run with it. Thanks, Dad. I'll go finish moving the boxes in now," Max told his dad and got up from the table.

His dad said, "I'll help." He started getting up from the table.

"No Dad, you know you can't help with your back. Mom would kill me," Max said, and then walked out of the kitchen, not giving George a chance to argue.

George sat at the kitchen table with a big grin on his face. He felt like a giddy little kid. He couldn't help but think Junie was going to love hearing about this and he couldn't wait until she called him that night to share the details.

♥ ♥ ♥

When Abby got home after being at her parent's house, she wondered if Colleen felt as horrible as she did as she popped two Ibuprofen, downed a glass of water, and then collapsed onto her couch. There was a reason Colleen was the only person in the world with whom she would have gone out the night before.

She was thankful Colleen had been there that awful day because she wasn't sure what she would have done without her. When Abby closed her eyes, it was like she was there again, experiencing the aftermath of Adam's decision. She couldn't stop the tears from welling in her eyes.

She knew she'd end up thinking about this night when she got home, even though she had put all of her energy lately into ignoring it, almost just as much energy as she put into the wedding plans.

She and Adam had fun booking the church and reception hall, going to cake and food tastings, choosing flowers, and sending out invitations. Although she did most of the planning, Adam helped with the main decisions and they got even closer while they planned their big day.

Abby had been adamant about not allowing Adam to see her wedding dress before the wedding because she didn't want to invite any bad luck before their big day. It was ironic to think of it now since it hadn't improved her luck. Instead of Adam, Colleen had gone with her to multiple dress shops to help choose Abby's wedding dress.

Everything was set for the wedding and the honeymoon in Florida was a trip they planned together. The day of their wedding Abby woke up happy and excited; her first thought that morning was to think that was the day she would become Mrs. Adam Jackson. She remembered lying in bed, thinking it was the happiest day of her life.

She would never forget any of the details of that day.

For months they played over and over in her head, like a broken record, wondering if she could have done anything to prevent it from happening.

One year earlier...

Abby had gotten up early that morning and had gone with Colleen to get their hair done by her hair stylist, who was also her good friend. She and Adam had decided weeks before they wouldn't see or talk to each other the day of the wedding until they met before the deacon at the altar.

After getting their hair done, Abby and Colleen had gone back to Abby's house to finish getting ready, but they still had a couple of hours before they had to be at the church so they were painting their toenails, chatting excitedly about the wedding and the honeymoon plans.

"I wish I could go with you to Florida. Do you think I'd fit in your suitcase? Or maybe I could go instead of Adam?" Colleen had asked, laughing.

"Hmm, I really don't think Adam would appreciate you going on our honeymoon instead of him. But I probably could manage to fit you in my suitcase if I unpacked all of my clothes," Abby replied back, laughing.

Right after that, the doorbell had rung. Abby remembered hobbling along with her newly painted toenails to answer it. She had been surprised to find Adam when she opened the door.

"Adam, you can't be here! It's supposed to be bad luck to see each other before the wedding."

Abby told Adam, trying to shut the door.

"Abby, wait." Adam's hand reached out to stop the door from closing. The look on his face warned her immediately that there was something very, very wrong.

"Adam, what's going on?" Abby asked him, opening the door back up.

"I can't do this. I'm sorry, Abby." He just stood there, looking at her. She just stood there, not yet understanding what he was trying to say.

"What do you mean, Adam?" Abby asked him, getting a sinking feeling in the pit of her stomach.

"I can't marry you today," Adam replied, refusing to look Abby in the eye.

Abby just stared at him for a minute. "You can't marry me...today? Is this a joke?" Abby asked, in a whisper.

Adam just stood there, staring at Abby, with tears welling up in his eyes, unable to talk. He took a deep breath to calm down.

Abby paused for a few moments, and then finally found her voice. "Are you saying you can't marry me today? Or ever?" Abby asked, starting to grasp what was happening.

Up to that point, Colleen had been standing quietly in the background, listening to the exchange, wondering what the hell had happened. She never in her wildest dreams thought this could happen with Adam and Abby. They were perfect for each other and were very happy!

She also deeply regretted the conversation she and Abby had right before the doorbell rang, wishing she could take back everything she had said. Oh, damn, did she jinx it for her best friend? Colleen shook off the guilt because she knew Abby needed her support.

She walked over to where Adam and Abby were talking and took Abby's hand, remaining silent.

Adam ignored Colleen and looked at Abby, wishing Colleen would disappear while he was choking out the hardest thing he'd ever had to do, but at the same time was glad she'd be there to support Abby.

"Last night I went to bed very happy, knowing I was going to become your husband today." Then Adam looked down at his feet because he couldn't look at her. "This morning, well, things are different."

Abby noticed Adam's hands were shaking. "Adam, why? What's going on?"

Abby saw the pain in his eyes and knew something had happened to make him change his mind, but didn't have any idea what it could be.

All Adam would say was, "I can't explain it right now."

"So, something happened all of a sudden to make you not want to marry me?" Abby said.

"Yes. No! It's not you at all! I do want to marry you. I just can't." Adam told her.

Abby was grasping at straws, and said, "Whatever it is, we can get through it. Just tell me what's going on. After that, we'll meet at the church and we'll get married at 4 o'clock just as we planned!" Abby tried to grab Adam's hand, but he pulled away.

"No, Abby, listen to me. I can't tell you what's going on and I can't marry you today." Adam told her a little more harshly than he intended.

"Is it another woman?" She asked him. She needed to know.

He hesitated just a little too long, and said "It's more complicated than that." He hated the look that came over her face at his explanation.

"Are you kidding me? This really isn't a joke?" Abby asked him.

He paused for a minute, softened his tone, and continued, "I have to go now. I booked a flight, and I'm on my way to the airport now. I'll call you when I get there."

"Where are you going?" Abby asked, completely shocked that he already had a flight booked taking him away from her and towards something or someone else.

Adam just shook his head, not willing to answer.

"I'll call you later. I'm sorry, Abby. I love you." Adam said, and then turned and walked quickly away, almost running.

Abby stood in the doorway, watching Adam leave, confused. She kept thinking he'd turn back around and laugh, saying just kidding! But no, he actually got in his car and drove away.

That's when Abby started to panic. What the hell was she supposed to do with the church full of people that would be waiting for them in a few hours? Would she have to go there and tell them what happened? Would she have to see the pity in people's eyes, wondering what she had done wrong to deserve this? How could she possibly explain to someone else what she didn't even understand herself?

29

What would her mom and dad say?

She turned toward Colleen and started breathing really hard, fear gleaming in her eyes.

Colleen finally spoke up, seeing the panic on her friend's face. "Talk to me, honey." Colleen was still holding her best friend's hand.

Abby started taking deep gulps of air, trying to calm down.

"I don't know what to say. I can't believe this is happening." She started to feel hot and very light-headed, so she started to wave her hands in her face, trying to cool herself off. Colleen sat her down on the couch and put Abby's head between her knees until she felt normal again.

When Abby sat back up, the first thing that came into her view was her beautiful wedding dress hanging up in the living room.

The dress was so pretty and it had made her feel so dainty when she tried it on in the store. She sat and stared at her dress, realizing she'd never get to wear it.

Although her breathing had finally gone back to normal, her resolve finally cracked and the tears started streaming down her face, smearing the perfectly applied makeup she had done just an hour and a half before. She put her head in her hands and sobbed. The man she loved and was supposed to marry had just left her, hours before the wedding.

Colleen just sat down next to her best friend, and rubbed her back, letting her get it all out. This went on for several minutes and then Abby stopped crying very suddenly.

"I don't have time to feel sorry for myself. I need to call my mom and dad.

Maybe they can help me tell everyone so I don't have to go to the church," She told Colleen in a panic.

"Do you want me to call your mom?" Colleen asked.

Abby answered her with her head down and said, "No, I need to do it." She picked up the phone and called her mom. Her mom answered the phone, and Abby wasted no time. "Mom, the wedding is off."

Abby's mom shrieked in her ear, "What?!?"

She took a deep breath and then explained what had happened.

"He did what?" Her mom asked angrily, and then said "I'm going to hunt that boy down and kick his sorry ass!" Her mom's reaction actually made her laugh at the same time as it brought fresh tears brimming in her eyes.

Abby's mom was not one for swearing or violence so it was strange, yet oddly comforting, to hear her say that.

"Thanks, Mom. Just don't beat him up too badly. No wait, never mind, have at it," Abby said.

She could hear her dad in the background, asking "What the hell is going on?"

Abby listened as her mom quickly explained to her dad what Adam had done, feeling like an eavesdropper listening in on a private conversation between her mom and dad about some woman who'd just been jilted. Then her mom told her dad to hush up so she could finish talking to Abby.

"I'll handle the phone calls, honey. Is Colleen still with you?" She asked, worried about her daughter.

"Yes, she's still here," Abby replied.

"Good. You need her right now," She said. Then, switched gears back to planning.

"I'll make the phone calls and then head up to the church to tell the deacon and wait for guests we can't reach. Luckily, only a few people are coming from out of town."

Yes, lucky, Abby thought.

"Thank you, mom," Abby told her mom.

"Oh honey, I'm so sorry. We'll get through this together, I promise. I love you. Dad wants to talk to you now, okay?" Her mom said, waiting for Abby's reply.

"Okay, mom. Thanks. I love you too," Abby replied, her eyes welling up again.

Abby's dad got on the phone next.

"Hi, honey. If there's anything you need your old man to do, let me know. I'm going to let your mom have the first crack at him and then I'll kick what's left of Adam's ass." It made her laugh again, just thinking

31

of her mom beating Adam to a bloody pulp. She could picture her mom slapping him silly while giving him a piece of her mind.

Shortly after the phone call to her parents, Adam's mom, Gina, called. She was extremely apologetic and told her she was very upset with her son. Abby and Adam's mom had gotten along very well, so it was no surprise to her when she told Abby she had "half a mind to disown her son".

She told Abby he had called her from the airport a few minutes ago and had told his mom the wedding was off but wouldn't tell her what was going on. Gina had tried to talk him out of it, but his mind was already made up. Gina promised to meet Abby's parents at the church to tell the people the wedding was off and told her not to worry about a thing. She also asked if Abby planned to go to Florida and Abby told her she hadn't thought about it yet.

Abby found it sad and ironic that something that had taken them a year to plan was unraveled in only a few hours, give or take a few remaining tasks that could wait until she returned from the honeymoon, she'd be taking by herself.

When she was done with everything, she needed to do to cancel the wedding she had poured her heart and soul into planning, she looked through the bags she had packed for the Florida honeymoon.

She started to realize she'd have to repack her bags because she wouldn't be taking some of the items she had already packed, like the negligees she had gotten at her bachelorette party the weekend before.

To muster the strength to repack, Abby looked up at Colleen with fire in her eyes and said, "Let's do a shot of tequila."

Colleen smiled, gave her a nod, and then went to do her task as quickly as possible. She grabbed two shot glasses, a bottle of Jose Cuervo, the salt, and the lemon from Abby's fridge. She placed it all on a tray and brought it to where Abby was sitting.

"Here we are, Abby." Colleen filled two shot glasses, passed Abby a lemon wedge, salted her hand after licking it, and then passed Abby the salt.

Abby followed suit and lifted up her shot glass and gave a toast. "To the honeymoon, I'll be enjoying alone in a few short hours."

Then, almost kiddingly, said, "Do you think you could go with me?" Abby looked up at her friend, shot in hand, the question in her eyes, hoping.

Colleen said, "Of course, I'll go with you!" and then lifted her glass and tapped it against Abby's. "To my best friend, we'll get through this, no matter how much alcohol this may take."

Abby managed a smile, asking, "Are you sure? Will Tom mind?"

"He'll be fine with it. Don't worry about it," Colleen replied. She knew her fiancé would be very understanding; that was just the sort of guy he was.

When that was settled, Abby and Colleen each slammed their shots, licked the salt, and sucked on the slice of lemon.

There were a couple more shots of tequila taken over the course of the next twenty minutes and Abby had to admit it was helping her by giving her a warm, fuzzy feeling to replace the confusion, anger, and hurt she had been feeling. She knew it would be very temporary, but she didn't care. Abby urgently wanted to go to Florida that night, but she didn't think they'd get a flight that quickly so she thought she'd get sloshed instead.

After Abby went into her bedroom to start the task of repacking for her very different trip, Colleen decided to give it her best shot and called the airport.

"Thank you for calling Sun Country. How may I help you?" The woman's voice spoke into the phone in her ear.

"Yes, hello. I really need your help. My best friend just had her heart broken." Colleen slurred into the phone.

Fortunately for them, she ended up speaking to a woman who recently had her heart broken and not only did they get their tickets switched to that night, they were upgraded to first-class seats.

Colleen then called the hotel and told them what had happened. She asked if they could check in early and switch from the honeymoon suite to a two-room suite. The hotel clerk told her to keep it secret but he comped them the extra night and said they'd have the new room ready when they got there. Everyone was very sympathetic to the situation, which helped, even if just a little bit.

33

The next call she made was for a taxi to come pick them up because neither of them was in any shape to drive. The last call she made was to her fiancé, Tom. She explained to him what Adam had done. Tom was shocked and told her Adam hadn't said a word to him, his own best man. Tom was glad to hear Colleen had agreed to go with Abby to Florida, and Colleen couldn't help but secretly thank her lucky stars for snagging the best man in the world.

Tom agreed to quickly pack her suitcase and bring it over to Abby's house. She told him she didn't much care what he packed as long as he packed her swimsuit, underwear, shorts, shirts, and her pills. Otherwise, she'd borrow what she needed from Abby. He quickly agreed to pack and bring it all within 20 minutes and she told him she loved him more than anything in the world.

When Abby came out of the room and Colleen told her everything she had arranged, Abby burst into tears and gave Colleen a huge hug for being the best friend a girl could possibly have.

Colleen stayed with her in Florida, and she had to admit they had several fun evenings. They also laid out by the pool every day and had come home with amazing tans.

Shortly after she came back from the honeymoon to Abby's surprise, Adam had called her. He then started to call her at least a couple times a week and sometimes he acted like nothing had happened. Other times he seemed very sad.

She had heard he was gone for just a couple of weeks and had returned back to his apartment. Abby had tried asking him what was going on several times, but she had never gotten an explanation from Adam.

She allowed him to call because at that time she had still hoped he would change his mind and they'd get married. She thought he'd eventually confide in her and tell her what was going on, but it just never came.

She eventually came to the conclusion he would never tell her and that hurt a lot that he couldn't trust her enough to tell her. She asked him each time he called what happened with a little more urgency because she was tired of waiting or a explanation for why he dumped her on her wedding day but he avoided the question. Each time he avoided it, it broke Abby's heart just a little more and it was another crack in the foundation they we supposed to have built.

She had heard through Tom and Colleen that he wasn't dating anyone, so it wasn't another woman, at least not anymore. She had to face the fact that he did not want to marry her.

After that realization, the next one came easily; she'd never get over Adam unless he stopped calling her and, for the sake of her sanity and well-being, she had to try.

Exactly two months after he left, Abby finally got up the nerve and asked Adam to stop calling. She remembered shaking and being very nervous but she was certain it was the right thing to do. It was a hard conversation that she had to just get through.

"Hi Abby, how are you?" Adam said.

"I'm fine. You?" Abby replied.

"I'm ok." Adam said, pausing, and then adding, "I miss you. I really want to see you." Adam told her.

It sounded like many of the other conversations they had. He always said he missed her and wanted to see her but never asked to come over or make plans to meet. Up until then, she had tried to ignore her instinct that he was saying those things to keep her hanging on.

Abby gripped the phone tighter and closed her eyes.

She took a deep breath and then said, "Adam, after two months you still haven't told me what happened. You haven't been honest and I can no longer wait for you to tell me, hoping that one day we'll eventually get married. I can't do this anymore."

Abby was relieved she finally had the courage to tell him how she felt.

Adam swallowed and asked her. "What are you saying, Abby?"

"Adam, I need to get on with my life and I can't do it while I still hold on to this foolish hope there's still a chance. I'm asking you to stop calling me. If you care about me at all, you'll respect my wishes," Abby told him.

There was a long pause, and Abby figured Adam was thinking. Finally, Adam said softly, "Okay."

Abby waited for a minute for him to say something else. When he was still silent, Abby asked "Okay? That's all you have to say? Still no explanation? Nothing?"

"Yes. Okay. It's only fair of you to ask me to stop calling. I understand and I don't blame you. I can't say I'm not disappointed, but I do understand. I won't call again. Before you go, please believe me when I say I do love you very much and I'm sorry I hurt you so badly. If I had a chance to do it all over again, things would have turned out very differently." Adam told her, and then said, "Goodbye, Abby."

Then Abby heard the dial tone. She looked at the phone in her hand, tears streaming down her face, and said, "Goodbye, Adam."

Why would he say that to her but not tell her what happened? She had told him so many times they couldn't get past this unless he was honest with her but he wouldn't ever tell.

To her relief, Adam respected her wishes and he hadn't called since.

For a while after their last conversation, every time the phone rang, she almost wished it would be him. That had been eight months ago. She was almost positive she saw him parked outside her pastry shop from time to time, but she wasn't completely sure because he never came inside.

♥ ♥ ♥

Abby opened her eyes and her thoughts quickly switched back to the present. She looked around her room, which she had redecorated twice since that fateful night.

The first time she painted the walls blue and had gotten a midnight blue bedspread. Blue was definitely the theme of her room, which matched her mood. After a while, her mood changed and she no longer wanted the blue walls or bedspread. She didn't want to be blue any longer so she had to change her room to something more cheerful.

She completely redecorated at that time using a pretty light green on the walls with a matching bedspread that had several different flowers with stems matching the green on her walls. The artwork she had still hung on her walls and both were painted by unknown artists; one was given to her by her grandmother before she died. It was of a mother feeding her children bread while they circled around her like little birds in a nest. The other was of a woman walking on the beach at sunset. Redecorating gave her something to do and she felt the different scenery would help her get over Adam a little faster.

Her thoughts suddenly switched to Max, wondering what his life was like and if his divorce felt anything like the pain, she felt the night she was supposed to have gotten married. She figured it was along the same lines because she had heard divorce was oftentimes worse than death, and for that, she was very sorry.

Chapter 3

Blind Dates Gone Wrong

*M*onday was her day off, and Abby had a date. She didn't just have a date; she was roped into a blind date by her parents. She had finally felt up to going on a few dates only recently.

Unfortunately, none of them had turned out so well, which seemed to be the theme her whole life. Other than Adam, she hadn't dated anyone for a long period.

Most of her dates had been friends of Colleen's fiancé, Tom, which was a little too weird for her since Adam was also his friend.

All she could do was picture all the guys talking to each other on poker night, talking about her with Adam. She found herself shuddering just thinking about it.

She couldn't help but laugh thinking about the most recent date she went just on a few weeks before. It was a man she had met grocery shopping; they had grabbed the same melon and touched hands. He seemed nice enough in the store but she should have known better when he refused to give up the melon, saying he'd found it first. She thought he was being flirty but after their date, she realized he would never have given up the perfect melon he had spent fifteen minutes picking out. She laughed out loud at the memory of that date. He had to read aloud the entire menu, twice, and then asked multiple questions of the waitress, and then changed his mind three times while he ordered.

She thought he had Obsessive Compulsive Disorder.

The date she was going on that night was with the son of a friend of her parents. She didn't want to go but had reluctantly agreed after being pestered for weeks by her mother. He was a paramedic and her mother said he was good-looking and very nice. Abby guessed it wouldn't hurt to go out.

At 7:00, Joe showed up at her door and she was pleasantly surprised that her mom was right; he was good-looking.

Maybe this would be a good date, after all, Abby thought.

"Hello, Abby. I'm Joe," He said, smiling at her while standing at her front door.

"Hi, Joe. Nice to meet you," Abby replied.

"Are you ready to go?"

"Yes, let's go," He told her. "Oh, hey, would you mind driving?" He added.

Well, that's odd. "Um, sure. I can drive," She replied.

"Great! Thanks. I was up all night and I am just a little tired tonight so I would rather not drive." He explained.

Okay, that made sense. "Oh, sure. I understand. Are you sure you want to go out tonight? If you were up all night, we could reschedule," She told him.

"Yeah, no worries! My mom would kill me if I bailed on you tonight. She's been bugging me for weeks," He told her, shaking his head. "Plus, my dad was right; you are hot!" He said and smacked her on the arm and laughed.

Hmm, she thought, he was a charmer, wasn't he?

"Okay. Let's go." The date wasn't starting so well, but she'd try to keep an open mind.

They hopped in her car, and then she started it up and pulled out of her driveway.

"Did you have somewhere in mind?" Abby asked Joe.

"Nah, not really. Anywhere with a bar," Joe answered and gave a little laugh.

Disregard the open mind; go to the nearest restaurant, have dinner, and call it a night. She didn't reply, just kept driving.

"So, you're a paramedic?" Abby asked, trying to make conversation with him. She already knew she didn't have much to go on.

"Yes," He answered, not offering anything more. "And you own a pie shop."

It was a little more than a pie shop, but she didn't care to correct him. "So, what do you do for fun when you're not saving someone's life?" She asked.

"Other than drinking? Well, maybe if you're lucky I'll show you later," Joe replied, wiggling his eyebrows in silent suggestion.

"Don't get your hopes up," Abby said under her breath and then gave up on the conversation.

Abby pulled into Applebee's parking lot and parked the car. When they got up to the door, she was surprised to have him open the door for her. Didn't seem to be in his character, but maybe she was too quick to judge.

When they got inside, before the Hostess could take them to a table, Joe raised his hand and said, "No, we want to eat at the bar so we can watch the Twins game." Then, as an afterthought, he turned to her and said, "Do you mind?" It wasn't a question because he didn't care either way, but at least he asked.

"I don't mind; I like watching baseball."

She replied. Abby was relieved a Twins game was on that night because it lessened the need for her to try to think of questions to ask him.

Joe ordered a Long Island Ice Tea and Abby ordered a glass of wine. When they ordered their meals, just as the game started, he also ordered another Long Island Ice Tea. Abby hadn't even taken a sip of her wine yet and he was done with his drink.

From that point on, they barely spoke and she had given up on trying to make conversation with him.

After dinner, they each paid their portion of the bill, and then Abby stood up to leave.

Joe said, "Don't you want to finish watching the game?" He looked at her like she was crazy.

"I have a very early morning tomorrow, so I need to get home," Abby replied, thankful for the excuse.

"How early? I thought I could come over after the game for a while," He said.

"Very early; I get up at 3:00 am," She told him. She couldn't ignore the second comment because there was no way in hell he was coming over. "And Joe, no, tonight doesn't work for you to come over."

Joe shrugged his shoulders. "Huh, okay. Well, I want to stay here and finish the game. Sit back down and relax," He said.

That's it, she was done. "Joe, I'm leaving. If you want a ride back to my house to get your car, you need to come now. If not, you'll need to get another ride," Abby told him with a hint of attitude.

"What? Give me a break! That wasn't a strike!" Joe was watching the TV and hadn't even heard her, so she repeated it, this time with more than a hint of an attitude.

"Joe! I'm leaving, NOW. If you want a ride back to my house to get your car, you need to come NOW. If not, you need to find a ride on your own." This time she had his attention.

"Oh, ok. Well, I guess I'll catch you later, Abby. I'll manage a ride back." Joe looked up at the pretty bartender, who had been giving him looks the entire 45 minutes they had been there.

Abby rolled her eyes and thought, be my guest.

"Okay then. Nice to meet you, Joe. Bye, bye."

Abby said and then walked out the door without looking back.

No more blind dates. She was done.

She jumped in her car and drove off towards home, thankful to have the date over and that she'd driven, but was left wondering when he'd pick up his car.

♥ ♥ ♥

Max and his dad went out for breakfast at "Dessert First" on Tuesday morning. They sat at a small table for two by a window, which was the place George and Junie usually would sit.

As they were waiting for their coffee and cinnamon rolls, George thought about the conversation he'd had with Junie two nights before, telling her about the conversation he'd had with Max about Abby.

Junie had giggled like a schoolgirl as he filled her in on their meeting and how awestruck Max seemed to be by her. George smiled at the memory.

He knew she'd get a kick out of it. If there was one good thing about her stroke, it would have to be that it brought Max home to them. If there were two good things, hell, even better, and he hoped it would be that it brought Max and Abby together.

"What?" Max asked his dad.

"What, what?" George asked in return.

"Why are you suddenly smiling?" Max asked his dad, suspicious.

"What? Can't a guy smile without getting the third degree?" George replied.

"Never mind, Dad," Max said, just looking at him, eyebrow raised.

A few minutes later, Abby walked out of the back room, noticed George at his usual table, and came right over to say hi.

"Mr. James! It's so nice to see you! You haven't been able to come in weeks." Abby glanced over at Junie's usual seat and found Max in place of her.

"Hello, Max," Abby said.

Max looked up at Abby and smiled. "Hi there, Abby. My dad told me all about this place and I wanted to come try one of your famous cinnamon rolls," Max said.

She looked back over at George, put her hand on his shoulder, and smiled. "Mr. James, you are much too kind."

Max couldn't help but think she was very cute in her apron, although he was pretty sure she'd be cute in just about anything…or nothing at all.

At that thought, Max turned red and was glad she wasn't looking at him.

"No Abby, you are much too good to us." George said to Abby, who turned to smile at Max.

"Well, boys, enjoy. I'd better get back behind the counter because I see we have a line going and Madeline needs some help." She turned back to George and said, "I have something totally new for you to try and I'll get you a piece to take home. I think you'll love it!"

Max couldn't help but notice Abby beaming at the thought of his dad trying her new dessert. He felt like his mom and dad had been very lucky to have gotten to know her over the years and he had missed out. He just wondered why they never mentioned any of this to him. It was all very surprising to Max.

"My mouth is watering already. See you later." George said.

As Abby was walking back behind the counter, a man at another table caught her attention and she walked over to his table. Max couldn't help but overhear the conversation.

"So, you're the owner?" The man asked Abby, eyes looking at her in hunger as if she were part of the meal. He had thick dark hair which was slicked back, he had a five o'clock shadow, and was wearing a very expensive suit. Although the man was handsome, he looked like he came right out of a mobster movie and gave her the creeps.

"Yes, sir. I hope you're finding your muffin to your satisfaction?" She replied to the man while he stared at her, another creepy shiver running down her spine.

"Oh, very much, but that's not why I called you over here. I was just wondering when I could take you out." The man replied. It wasn't said as a question, but rather like he was stating a fact, showing just how arrogant he was.

She paused for a moment, trying to keep calm. The last thing she wanted was to upset a customer or other customers and give her place a bad name. She took a deep breath and then said calmly, "I'm seeing someone, so I'm afraid that won't be possible. Please enjoy the rest of your breakfast," Abby told him and walked towards the kitchen before he could say another word.

She was asked out by customers once in a while and understandably always said no. There was no way she'd get into a relationship with someone the same way she had with Adam; she felt it was not the kind of luck she wanted. This guy seemed like a creepy arrogant jerk, so she had no regrets about saying no to him.

Abby shook it off and went back behind the counter to help Madeline.

"Now who is that over there you were talking to, then?" She asked Abby.

"Some creepy guy who asked me out. No thanks," Abby replied shuddering while suppressing her smile. Abby knew full well Madeline was referring to Max.

"Oh, you stop that, now," Madeline replied. "You know who I'm talking about, deary."

"Oh, him! That just so happens to be the boy who I used to have a crush on growing up.

Max James," Abby replied.

"Oh? You never mentioned him to me before," Madeline scolded.

"Well, there's no reason to mention him, really," Abby said.

"Well, if you ask me, he's certainly worth mentioning!" Madeline said.

Abby had already filled Madeline in on her less-than-fantastic date the night before with Joe. More annoying was that Joe's car was still in her driveway when Abby had left for work that morning. She had halfway thought about getting it towed! With that date behind Abby, Madeline was eager to move on to the next possibility and already had Max in her sights.

Abby shook her head at Madeline and then started to prepare George's take-home box with the new dessert she wanted George to try.

She thought for a minute and then decided to stick in an extra serving in case Max wanted to try it too.

Once she saw that George and Max were finished with their breakfast, Abby walked over to their table and set down the to-go box in front of them, giving them a big smile. The two men looked down at the box and sat back down. Max thought if it was anything like the grasshopper bars they had tried on Sunday, he'd be in heaven.

George couldn't help but take a peek at what was inside the box and when he opened it, both of their mouths watered. Inside the box looked to be a very delicate pastry with lemon filling and topped with real whipped cream. It looked so amazing, George and Max looked at each other and smiled, both nodding in silent agreement.

George picked up his fork and took a bite. She knew from experience that his smile was his seal of approval so when she saw the smile appear on his face after the first bite, she couldn't help but smile in return.

Abby was laughing as she walked away to wipe off a counter and leave them for their dessert, which she had intended for them to take home. Abby couldn't help but glance over at Max as he took his first bite. As soon as the tart hit his tongue, he was hooked. It was lemony and flaky and buttery and melted in his mouth. He thought the cinnamon roll had been good, but this was amazing. He looked up at her and caught her eye.

"Do you like it?" She asked hesitantly.

"Like it? No," Max replied, and he watched her beautiful face fall ever so slightly. "I love it. It's delicious!" He told her.

She smiled at him and said "Thanks".

George said, "Girl, this is a keeper."

She beamed at George and told him "I knew you'd like it, George. As for Max, I wasn't so sure. I don't know him like I know you."

"Are you kidding? I can't believe this is something you cooked up. You're amazing! I liked those grasshopper bars, too," Max said. Abby blushed. She could feel her body's temperature rise and her cheeks heat up.

"Well, I guess I'll let you two eat the rest of the dessert now. I'm glad you liked it," Abby said and got up from the table.

"Abby, wait. I was wondering about that dinner we discussed a few days ago. Would you be free Friday night?" Max asked.

"Friday night I usually work late doing inventory and bookwork," Abby replied.

He was asking her out! She couldn't believe it.

"Saturday night?" Max asked, hopefully.

"Sorry, I already have plans," Abby replied, thinking of the plans she had with Colleen Saturday night. She was sure Colleen would understand, but she wasn't sure if she could go out with Max.

She thought about all the pranks his friends played when she was a kid, especially the night they told her Max wanted to go on a date with her. Plus, her heart melted each time she saw him and she didn't trust it.

"I guess another time," Max replied. Even though she showed no interest, he wasn't going to give up that easily.

"Yes, another time," Abby replied. "Enjoy the rest of your day, gentlemen." She walked away from the table wondering if she had made the right decision with turning him down for a date.

Max looked over at his dad and shrugged his shoulders.

On the way home, Max said to George, "I tried, right?"

"Give her some time, Max," George said. "I didn't share this with you earlier but I'll tell you now. About a year ago, Abby was engaged to a man. On the day of their wedding, he told her he couldn't go through with it. He left her with a broken heart and a mess to clean up."

"That's rough," Max said, shaking his head and wondering how someone could leave a woman like Abby. His heart had been broken too, so he felt like he knew what she was going through. His heart was still mending, even years after his divorce.

"Give it time and ask again," George repeated. George was disappointed she had said no, but he hoped his son didn't give up that easily.

♥ ♥ ♥

Abby finished for the day, cleaned the kitchen, and then headed home with a piece of her tasty new dessert for a late-night snack to eat while she watched a movie. She could never go to bed right away. As she drove home, she thought about the creepy man who had asked her out.

She later found out he had left his number for her at the front counter, asking Madeline to give it to her. She promptly ripped it up and threw it in the trash bin, hoping he never came back to her shop.

Abby got home, popped in "Bridget Jones Diary", one of her favorite chick flicks, and sat down with her dessert. She couldn't help but wonder what Max was doing. It was such a different scenario, having him asking her out. She wasn't sure how to handle it. Did she want to go out with him? Hell yes!

She was just afraid. She was glad to be going out with Colleen that weekend; she'd have some good advice for Abby.

On the other side of town, Max was sitting in bed, trying to fall asleep and he was thinking of Abby. He was trying to remember how he treated her growing up and couldn't remember much about her other than her staring a lot. She didn't seem the least interested in him now, unfortunately. He smiled to himself and thought he was determined to change that.

♥ ♥ ♥

Abby's week flew by. Friday night, she took inventory, did her bookwork and payroll, and then finished cleaning up the shop. She packed up all of the donuts and pastries that she hadn't sold for that week, which ended up being about two boxes of cakes, donuts, and other yummy desserts.

She usually brought the leftovers to various places where they were sure to be appreciated. One place was the Seniors' home in Elk River, Guardian Angels. Her grandmother used to live there until she died two years before and the seniors had loved the pastries so much, she tried bringing them leftovers at least once a month. Another place was the small orphanage near St Cloud. Her heart broke every time she went there, but at least she brought the kids a little treat each week.

One day, she vowed, she would adopt a child; it was just something she always wanted to do. The last place she brought the leftovers was to the library. She figured there would be workers and patrons who would love a donut or something while reading a book and drinking coffee.

It was also a great way to advertise because the library patrons also ended up coming in to buy things after trying something at the library. It was a win-win and a great business decision.

She didn't want it to go to waste and giving it away meant it never did.

After she left the shop, she dropped off one of the boxes of pastries at the orphanage and the other at the library and then headed home and went to bed.

Saturday morning, she woke up at 3:00 am and took a shower. Madeline was going to meet her that morning to start baking to get ready for the weekend.

After she made it to the shop, she went in the back door and found Madeline was already there, starting to set up the ingredients needed for baking that morning. She loved Madeline and couldn't imagine running her business without her.

"So, anything new on that neighbor?" Madeline asked.

"Max? Not much is new. I haven't seen him since he was here earlier this week," Abby told her.

"Hmm, you should ask him out," Madeline said. "He's very good-looking and seemed very sweet."

"Yes, well, I don't think so," Abby replied. Then she noticed Madeline's raised eyebrow and she amended what she said, "I mean, yes, he's very good-looking, but I'm not sure about the very sweet thing. He and his friends used to torture me when I was growing up."

"Torture you?" Madeline asked, skeptically.

"Well, what do you call playing pranks and jokes on a kid three years younger?" Abby asked.

"I call that being boys," Madeline said, knowing exactly what she was talking about considering she had children of her own.

"Well, I call it mean," Abby said. Changing the subject, she said, "When are you going to go out on a date with that guy who comes in here pining over you?"

"Charles? I'm not. I can't ever go out with anyone again. I've lived my life. Now, I'm helping you with yours," She replied.

"Hmm, well, he's one handsome man who is definitely interested in you," Abby said.

"Well, we're friends. That's it," Madeline answered. Then, she changed the subject. "Do you want me to make a fresh pan of grasshopper bars? Or will it be toffee bars this week?"

"Toffee bars since we had the grasshopper bars last week," Abby told her. "And I decided it's been too long since we made lemon muffins. Doesn't that sound good?" Abby's famous lemon muffins were amazing; the lemon rind is grated into a batter of sugar, eggs, cream, and flour, and the lemon juice is poured on top of the cooled muffins to make them extra lemony and tart.

"Everyone loves those lemon muffins of yours. Did you already have the lemons delivered this week?" Madeline asked her.

"Yup! And the cream, too" Abby said.

"Well, let's get to work, shall we?" Madeline asked, which was her cue to crank up the music and get cooking.

♥ ♥ ♥

After baking all morning, Abby set out the fresh bars, cookies, muffins, and donuts in the display case. She also prepared some samples for people to try since she found nothing sold as well as when she offered samples.

A few hours after opening, she left the shop in the capable hands of Madeline and her Saturday crew. She was excited to go out with Colleen that night but wanted to be able to take a nap before she did.

Abby and Colleen were planning to go to dinner and a movie in Elk River. Going to the movies was always their favorite thing to do. They loved comedies the best, although they'd see almost anything together and have fun doing it. They often laughed through an entire movie, getting stares from other movie-goers. Their favorite routine was to go to Buffalo Wild Wings to have wings and a few drinks. Then, they would go see a movie at the theater right next door to let the drinks wear off before they had to drive home.

At precisely 7:00 pm, Colleen drove up Abby's driveway and honked the horn. As Abby walked towards the car, she could see Colleen checking her lipstick in the rear-view mirror. Abby smiled to herself, thinking how she had just done that in her entryway mirror before Colleen showed up.

As Colleen drove them towards the direction of the theater, Abby told Colleen about the surprise her parents had for her the other night.

"Abby, that's fantastic! You'll be in heaven! I wish I could go with you, but I guess I'll be a little busy on my honeymoon." Colleen told her, smiling.

"Yes, I wish you could go too, but I'm also looking forward to spending time doing exactly what I want to do for 10 whole days," She told her friend.

"Maybe you'll meet someone there," Colleen said, raising her eyebrows.

"Hmm, maybe," Abby replied, thinking about Max, wondering if a relationship with him would go anywhere if she ever agreed to go out with him. "Colleen, you'll never guess who I ran into the other day."

"Who?" Colleen asked.

"Max James," Abby replied, knowing Colleen would immediately get what that meant for her.

"Oh, my God! Are you serious? What did he look like? What did he say?" Colleen asked. She wanted all of the juicy details.

"Well, he looks good," Abby said, not telling Colleen that she thought he was hot as hell. "He said he moved back to town to help take care of his parents."

"Well, that's sweet of him. Is he back for good?" Colleen asked, her mind already racing a mile a minute. Abby needed to move on with life after Adam, and wouldn't it be ironic if it ended up being her old crush that helped her do just that?

"Yes, I guess so. It sounded like he'd live with his parents for a while and then look for a place of his own," Abby replied, amazed at how quickly they had made it to the theater.

Colleen parked the car at the theater. They usually parked near the theater and walked the short distance over to the bar.

"What else did he say?" Colleen asked as she got out of the car.

"Well, he asked me out," Abby said, getting out of the car and shutting the door.

"Really? When are you going out?" Colleen asked, excited.

"I turned him down," Abby told her.

"You did what?!?" Colleen asked her, wondering what the hell her friend was thinking.

"I have no desire to go out with him. He wanted nothing to do with me growing up, so why go out now?" Abby asked her.

"Well, gee, Abby, let's see. You were only 15 when we went away to college, still just a little girl. He ignored you because a three-year difference is a lot when you're that young.

Now? Not so much! You should go for it! You pined over him as a kid!" She told her, having a hard time understanding why Abby would turn him down.

"Yes, exactly, and I don't need to be reminded of that," Abby replied sarcastically.

They walked in the door of Buffalo Wild Wings and chose a booth in the restaurant area but still very close to the bar.

The booths had very high backs so no one could see them but they both had a pretty good view of the people in the bar.

Abby scanned the bar to see if she knew anyone and she gasped in surprise. Right there, only ten feet away, was Max James sitting at a table with another guy.

Abby turned her head slightly to see if she could tell who it was and was disappointed to find Max with Pete, the person who just happened to be the one who used to pull the meanest jokes and took the most advantage of Abby's crush. She should have figured he'd still be friends with Pete. Abby's stomach lurched and felt her desire to try dating Max go even further downhill. She hit Colleen and pointed to the table.

"Col, Max is here!" Abby told her.

"What?!?! Where?" Colleen asked, whispering back. What luck! Maybe they could talk to him.

"Right over there, first table in the bar," Abby replied, still whispering.

"That's Max? Oh my God, he's hot!" Colleen said loudly. "Why the hell would you say no to him?"

"Shush!!" Abby told Colleen. "He'll hear you."

Just then the waitress came up and took their drink order. They each ordered a lemon drop martini to get the night started. After the waitress left, they turned their attention back to the men.

"Be quiet. Let's see if we can hear them," Colleen said.

Max turned his head toward a table in the restaurant because he could have sworn he heard his name. He shrugged it off and thought he was going crazy. He turned back towards Pete, who had called him up out of the blue and asked him to have a beer and catch up. They had gotten to the bar just a few minutes before Abby and Colleen and Max had no idea they were there.

51

Colleen and Abby listened for a minute and realized little they could hear the conversation perfectly.

"Pete. It's good to see you. It's been years," Max said.

As Abby heard Max's comment, she realized Max and Pete were catching up. She was a little relieved to learn they didn't hang out anymore.

As Max listened to Pete, he found out most of the guys they used to hang out with were married and had kids and some, like him, were divorced. It made him feel old.

"Speaking of friends, do you remember Abby, my neighbor growing up?" Max asked Pete.

"Oh, yeah, I remember her. She had a major crush on you, man." He snickered at the memories, thinking it had been so easy to tease the girl and get her to do just about anything if it involved Max at all.

"Have you seen her recently?" Max asked, wondering if he ever ran into Abby since he still lived around here.

"Nah, I haven't seen her in years," Pete replied.

"I saw her the other day," Max told him.

"No kidding? Still, the lanky girl she used to be?" Pete asked, thinking she hadn't been much of a looker growing up so she couldn't be much now. "Or did she get fat or something?" Pete started laughing at the thought.

"Actually, she's smokin' hot," Max replied, feeling proud to be able to stick up for Abby.

Abby blushed as she heard Max tell Pete she was hot and Colleen reached over the table and smacked her in the arm.

"Ouch!" Abby whispered and let a giggle escape her lips, thinking she felt bad for eavesdropping, but couldn't believe what she was hearing and couldn't stop listening.

Colleen put a finger to her lips and told her to hush up. Their drinks had arrived and they both took a sip of their lemon drop martinis. Then, they turned their ears back toward the men at the bar.

"What? You're putting me on," Pete said, laughing, thinking surely Max had lost his mind. It was part of why he always teased her; she just wasn't very attractive.

"Seriously. Our parents all still live next to each other so I ran into her. She's pretty damn hot," Max told him. Pete was a jerk and sometimes Max wondered why he ever hung out with him in school, but it was mostly because he felt sorry for Pete. He had been a bit of a chubby kid and was picked on growing up.

They became friends the year after he had moved to Minnesota when Max told others to leave Pete alone.

However, he never understood why Pete still picked on others. Max figured it was probably to make himself feel better, but thought Pete, of all people, should know how it felt.

"Huh, that's funny. Can't picture it. But hey, if she's hot, you going to go after her? If not, mind if I hit that? My wife wouldn't have to know," Pete said, laughing and shaking his head.

"Shut up, Pete," Max told him, remembering exactly why he had stopped hanging out with him.

Pete went on. "Hell, we tortured her when we were growing up, even after you left.

Bet she wouldn't give us the time of day now," Pete said.

Max looked confused, ignoring Pete's comment about going after Abby. "What are you talking about? We barely ever talked to Abby when we were younger."

Abby and Colleen looked at each other, raised their eyebrows, and then looked back at the two men. They couldn't wait to hear Pete explain.

"You don't remember? How about the time I told her you were waiting by the pool, knowing you had Rebecca there? It was perfect timing because Abby walked back there just as Rebecca was kissing you. We all knew Abby had a major crush on you and she did exactly as we thought she would and ran away in tears." Pete was laughing hysterically as if it were the most hilarious thing in the world.

Max looked at him, surprised. "What? Why would you send her back there?"

"It was so easy to get her going. Gave us a good laugh," Pete said and then kept going, ignoring the look on Max's face.

"We used to convince her to do your chores so we could go out. I always told her one of those times we'd let her come with us but we never did. I always wondered how far she'd let us go.

Sometimes we'd have her walk to the store to get us snacks for the pool, and she'd use her own money! We told her we'd pay her back but never did. She was so dumb," Pete said, still laughing.

"What the hell are you talking about?" Max said, getting angrier as Pete kept going on.

Had he been oblivious to all of that? "She wasn't dumb, you ass. She was just a kid!"

Pete ignored Max, not realizing how angry he was, still laughing like a hyena. "The best was the time I told Abby you wanted to take her out on a date. I told her you were too shy to ask her out so she should just get ready and you'd pick her up." Pete began. Max just sat there with a frown, listening and wondering what Pete had done next.

Pete continued, laughing. "Rick and I were in on that one and we saw her waiting on her front porch in a dress and she had her hair done." Pete continued. "We were laughing at her while you drove us away," Pete said, shaking his head, slapping his knee, and laughing hysterically.

"You had asked us what was so funny back there and even looked back at her sitting there and you had no idea she was waiting for you." He was laughing so hard, there were tears in his eyes. Pete was oblivious to the fact that Max was furious.

Max just sat there, processing what he had heard. He vaguely remembered a time when he had seen Abby all decked out. He remembered wondering where she was going all dressed up.

"What the hell, Pete? I told you to leave her be! She was just a kid. What the hell?" Max repeated.

He downed his beer, motioned for the bartender to get him another, and downed that one too. He had to do something since he was ready to punch out the guy, he used to consider his friend. He was starting to see why Abby wanted nothing to do with him.

They hadn't seen each other in years and he never could put a finger on why he stopped hanging around Pete, but maybe in the back of his mind, he always knew the guy was an ass. Now he knew for sure.

What was worse was Pete was still laughing about it. The guy hadn't changed at all. How Pete could be married, Max wasn't sure. A woman would have to be crazy to be with someone like Pete.

From where Abby was sitting, Max looked and sounded pissed off. With his fist curled up, he looked like he was about to punch his friend. Abby looked at Colleen, eyes wide open.

Neither of them could believe what they were hearing!

Abby realized she had been holding a slight grudge against Max, thinking he somehow knew what was going on but had ignored it or worse yet, was part of it. Now she knew the truth. Abby could feel her wall breaking down as she continued to listen to their conversation.

There was silence for a while as Max was trying to control his anger. Finally, he said to Pete, "How did I not notice any of this?"

Abby heard Pete reply to Max, "you told us to leave her alone but it was way too much fun. We just never let you see what we were doing, but we always thought you sort of knew." Pete finally realized Max was genuinely pissed off and started to chug his beer, thinking he better high-tail it out of there since Max was such a downer.

"Hell no, I didn't know. No wonder she has no interest in going out with me. You're an ass, you know that? How the hell did you ever manage to get married? She's a saint to put up with you, man," Max told him, calming down a little. The beer was helping, although he'd have to slow down if he'd ever be able to drive home tonight. Maybe tonight was a night to call his dad to pick him up.

"Dude, calm down. Big deal! It was thirteen years ago, man. It was fun to tease her," Pete said to Max.

Abby couldn't believe her ears. Max wasn't a part of what happened all those years ago.

Max didn't stand her up. He didn't expect her to do his chores and he was never part of what those guys did over the years. She really should have known. They even continued to play a few tricks on her after Max had left but since Max wasn't around, it wasn't as much fun because she no longer fell for their tricks and they stopped shortly after he left. She had been thankful they had finally given up.

Abby and Colleen ordered another martini and some hot wings and sat in silence while they waited.

"I gotta split, man," Pete told Max, and then got up, leaving Max sitting there by himself drinking a beer, shaking his head.

Colleen finally broke the silence, whispering, "You should walk up to the bar and then notice him sitting there."

"No way! What if he finds out we heard the whole conversation?" Abby asked in a whisper back to Colleen.

"How would he? Just go! Guzzle your next martini and then do it." Colleen urged.

The martinis miraculously arrived just at that moment. Before she could lose her nerve, Abby picked up the drink, downed it in two gulps, and then got up from the table. Liquid courage was an amazing thing.

Abby sauntered up to the bar, walking right past Max. She was hoping he would notice her, but he was looking down at his beer bottle. So, she drummed up the courage and in a fake surprised voice asked, "Max? Is that you?"

Max looked up from his beer in surprise, thinking it was a coincidence that she was standing there when he had been talking about her only moments before. "Hey, Abby, how are you? Who are you with?" Max asked, looking around the bar, wondering if she was on a date.

"I'm with Colleen. We're sitting right over there." Abby pointed to their booth.

Max's eyes widened in surprise, wondering if there was any way she could have heard the conversation he'd just had with Pete. He dismissed the idea and thought he was being crazy.

"We're having a couple of drinks and then heading over to the theater to see a movie," Abby told Max. "You're welcome to join us if you want," Abby said before she even thought about it.

Max smiled at Abby and told her, "I'd like to, but I have an early morning tomorrow." It wasn't exactly his idea of a first date if they wouldn't be alone.

"Okay, maybe another time," Abby told him, giving him an opening.

"Well, how about setting something up now? You said Fridays aren't good for you, right?" Abby nodded, surprised he remembered her schedule. "How about next Saturday?" Max asked.

Abby paused for a minute and then decided to go for it. "Saturday would work," She replied.

"Great!" Max agreed, his blue eyes sparkling. "Can I get your number? I'll give you a call this week."

Abby gave him her number and then got up from the table to head back to Colleen, who she was sure was dying for details, even though she knew very well Colleen could hear everything they were saying. "I'd better get back to Colleen. Have a great night."

"You too, Abby. Have fun at the movie," Max replied.

He stood up to leave and noticed the check. Max shook his head, not surprised at all that Pete had left him with the bill. Max placed forty dollars on the table, and despite that, he left the bar with a huge smile on his face.

♥ ♥ ♥

The following week went by very slowly for Max, much to his frustration. He unpacked and helped make preparations for his mom to come home from the hospital. They thought it would be sometime the following week when she'd be released, although the doctors were still worried about her dizzy spells.

George was worried but tried not to show it.

They were both getting up there in age, although they weren't that old.

George and Junie were older when they had Max. The doctors had told them they couldn't have kids. Junie proved them wrong when she was 40 and got pregnant with their one and only child. They were three years apart, just like Max and Abby. They were still very much in love and George took it very hard when she had her stroke.

Max was looking forward to Saturday but didn't really know what to plan for their date. He wanted to impress her by taking her to a nice restaurant and then for something special afterward but wasn't sure where they'd go yet. He had time, he knew, but he wanted her to have fun.

Tuesday evening, he called Abby to confirm their plans.

He had finally figured out where he was going to take Abby.

The phone rang three times and then she answered the phone, breathlessly.

"Hi Abby, it's Max. Busy?" He answered.

"Hi Max. No, I'm not busy," Abby replied, looking around her kitchen, which looked like it had been destroyed in a tornado. She decided to clean out one drawer and the next thing she knew, the entire kitchen was being ripped apart. She had the contents of all cupboards in her kitchen on the table and the center island, waiting to be put back into their freshly cleaned space.

"Are you still up for Saturday night?" He asked, trying not to sound too hopeful, but he would be very disappointed if she had changed her mind.

"Yes," She replied and thought it was so weird to be talking to him on the phone. She hoped she didn't regret this.

"Good. I was thinking I'd pick you up at 6:00 for dinner," He replied, hoping it wasn't too early.

"Works for me. Where are we going?" She asked, and then quickly added. "I just wondered how I should dress."

"Casual. I was hoping we could eat somewhere outside and enjoy the weather. Is that okay with you?" Max asked Abby.

"I end up being stuck inside a lot of the time; being outside sounds perfect," Abby replied, a smile on her face.

"Good. I'm looking forward to Saturday, Abby." Max was hoping they would spend the whole evening together and was planning to take her to a casual restaurant where they could eat on the patio and then go to a concert in the park.

In Minnesota, you didn't even know what the weather would be like. One day it could be 90 degrees and sunny and the next could be 45 degrees and cold as ice.

He was hoping for a good day.

The conversation was a little awkward. "Me, too," Abby said.

"So, where do you live?" Max asked her.

Abby gave him her address.

"You don't live far at all," He commented.

"No. I didn't want to move too far away from my parents so I can visit often. I drop in to see your parents once in a while too," Abby added.

"Yes, I heard about that. Sounds like you've treated them very well over the years. I'm jealous," Max said.

"I really like your parents so I enjoy visiting with them," Abby said. "Well, I better run. I have to get ready for work in a little bit and have some errands to run in town."

"Okay. I'll see you Saturday, Abby," Max said.

"See you then, Max," Abby said, and gently hung up the phone.

She sat there for a while looking at the phone.

She had spoken to Max only one other time in her life on the phone and it was an embarrassing memory. Her mom had made her call to borrow a cup of sugar. Abby was mortified when he answered the phone and she stuttered out "C-C-Could I p-p-p-please speak with Mrs. J-J-James?"

All he had said was "Hold on a sec." and then he handed the phone over to his mom. She wondered if he'd even remember and hoped not.

Chapter 4

Date with Dad

On Wednesday morning, Abby's dad picked her up for one of their frequent fishing excursions. It was one of her favorite things to do with her dad and she'd been doing it since she was a little girl. They talked, laughed, and on occasion, even cried.

She tried to go with him at least once a month from the fishing opener in May up to the end of September, depending on the weather. Abby's dad fished all year long, but she wouldn't fish unless it was in open water. There was nothing that could get her out to fish on the ice in the dead of winter; the cracking ice freaked her out and she was terrified of drowning in the ice-cold water.

"Hi, Dad! You ready to catch some walleye?" Abby asked him, excited to get out on the water early that morning.

"I hear they're catching 'em on the north end of the lake today so we'll head over there and see if they're lying," John told her. He enjoyed fishing with his daughter. She sometimes managed to out-fish him, which always made him proud.

"Well, let's go then!" She told him.

Her dad started driving and then said "I ran into Max yesterday. He sure seems like a nice fellow, Abby," He told her.

"What did he say?" Abby asked, wondering if he had mentioned their upcoming date. She sort of doubted he'd say anything to her dad.

"He told me about his mom and that she's doing better, but still not ready to come home. George sure misses Junie," He told her, thinking how he'd feel if that had happened to Sandy, Abby's mom.

"I know. I saw him last week and he mentioned her a couple of times. It must help to have Max here, but I'm sure he misses her very much," She told her dad.

"Max mentioned you two are going to go out this weekend," Her dad told Abby.

She was surprised Max would have said anything to her dad. "Yes, well, I ran into him the other night when I went out with Colleen." Not explaining further.

"Hey, speaking of dates, what happened with Joe the other night? Did you have a good time?" Her dad asked her.

She gave her dad a warning look. "Do you want the truth or would you rather I say I had a great time?" She asked.

"That good, huh?" Her dad looked disappointed, but not exactly surprised. "What happened?"

"Nothing much, really, other than he got smashed at the restaurant, and because the Twins were on, he wouldn't leave. So, I left him there and went home. I'm sure he got a ride home from the bartender who kept staring at him the whole 45 minutes we were there together," Abby told her dad.

"Well, that sounds fun," Her dad replied sarcastically.

"I'm pretty sure he was forced to go out with me and hated every minute." Abby just shook her head at the memory.

"Oh. I thought he sounded like a decent guy, being a paramedic and all." He thought for a moment and said "Guess we've failed at enough dates for you. I think we'll hang up that hat now," Her dad said, chuckling.

"Can you please be sure to let Mom know?" Abby asked him, laughing and rolling her eyes. She knew full well it was her mom, not her dad, who kept coming up with people for her to date. She couldn't stand the thought that Abby still hadn't found anyone to replace Adam.

"Will do, honey," Her dad said and then patted her on her shoulder. "Not sure if she'll listen, but I'll try."

They had gotten to the boat launch shortly after that conversation and they worked quickly to get the boat in the water. They had done it so many times together that they made it look very easy.

Abby got the boat running and then drove it to one of the docks at the launch, waiting for her dad to park the truck and trailer. She sat in the boat for a few minutes, wondering what her date with Max would be like. She wondered where he may take her.

Her dad made it to the dock, hopped in the boat, and drove them out to the spot where they were supposedly catching fish. There were several boats already there when they got to the location.

"Lines in," Her dad said. It was his way of telling her to drop her line and catch a big one.

Abby didn't say anything, but took her pole out of the storage under the seats, expertly put on a shiner, and dropped her line in. Not a minute later, she had a bite.

Abby and her dad fished for a few hours and caught their limit of crappie, which was their favorite fish to eat besides Walleye.

Abby was glad to be with her dad on that beautiful day. As her dad would always say, it was a good day to be alive.

♥ ♥ ♥

On Friday morning, she had an appointment to get her hair done by her friend, Krista, who worked at Belli-Capelli in Andover. Krista had been a friend since high school and when she became a hair stylist, Abby was one of her first customers. She'd been going to her for years and couldn't wait for every appointment.

As Abby walked in the door of the salon holding two white chocolate mochas from Caribou Coffee, several people said hello to her. She was there fairly often and loved the atmosphere of the shop. She couldn't think of a better way to spend a morning off than to pamper herself, whether it was to get her hair cut and colored, to get wax and facial, to get a mani/pedi, or to get a massage. Coming to the salon was something she always looked forward to doing and that day was no exception.

"Here you are, ma'am," Abby told Krista. It had become a tradition to bring her a white chocolate mocha when she came in. She liked to pamper the person who took such good care of her.

Krista's eyes widened, she grabbed the coffee from Abby's hand and took a large gulp. When she had swallowed the coffee, Krista said, "Thank you! I needed one of these today. I'm tired, as usual, but more so today."

"Baby keeping you up all night?" Abby asked her.

"Yes, and so is my 2-year-old! They take turns waking me up. Sarah will just get back to sleep and then Nathan wants his blanket or his nuk. I love it, don't get me wrong, but I could use just a tad more sleep," Krista told her. She had just had their second child four months before and was having a hard time adjusting to the lack of sleep. As strange as it was to say, Abby was a little jealous.

"Does Jason help you out?" Abby asked her.

"Yes, he's very good about it so unfortunately, we both have a lack of sleep on our resume at the moment. It will get better, I know, but it's hard. So, thank you for this," Krista said and then paused as she took a sip, a little smaller this time. "It'll be a lifesaver today."

"You are very welcome," Abby told her and then sat down in her chair.

"So, what are we doing today? Are you ready to go lighter blonde again? Maybe cut a few layers to pull out your curls a little?" Krista asked.

It amazed Abby that every time she walked into the salon Krista knew exactly what she wanted to do with her hair. She had a gift; Abby was sure of it.

"Exactly what I was thinking, Krista. How do you do it?" Abby asked.

"I just know you. So, any special occasion or just doing this for yourself?" Krista asked her.

"Both, actually," Abby said, and then asked Krista, "Do you remember Max James from high school? He was three years older than us?"

"Yes, I remember. He was hot!" Krista told her. "Why?"

"I ran into him the other day. We're going out tomorrow night," Abby replied with a little smile on her face.

"Really? That's great! Didn't you always have a huge crush on him? I thought he moved away," Krista said, remembering how heartbroken her friend had been when Max had left for college.

"He did, but he's back now to help take care of his parents. It's been thirteen years," Abby said.

"Has it been that long? That makes me feel old," She replied, giving a huge sigh.

"Tell me about it," Abby told her.

"So? Is he still hot?" Krista asked, thinking he couldn't possibly have gotten ugly because he was the hottest senior in high school when they were freshmen. She sighed dreamily.

"He's pretty good-looking, I'd have to say. He seems nice, too," Abby told her.

"Well, I want all the juicy details. I have to live through others for a while. All Jason and I can do at night lately are pass out as soon as we have the kids in bed," Krista told her.

"Okay, I'll let you know how it goes," Abby told her.

Krista walked away to mix up the color and Abby sat there, enjoying her coffee. Krista was the one who had fixed her hair and did her makeup on her wedding day and was mortified when she found out Adam had left her. Adam used to see her as well, but she fired him from being her client in support of Abby. She had told Krista she didn't have to do that, but Krista wouldn't hear of seeing him after he had done that to Abby.

When Krista got back to her station with the color and foils, Abby asked her, "Hear any good gossip lately?"

"Well, let's see. Did you hear Mr. Carlson, our English teacher in high school, got a Senior pregnant this year?" Krista told her.

"No! How did you find out?" Abby asked her.

"My cousin is a Senior this year," Krista told her. "Isn't that gross? He must be 60 years old!"

"At least! That is gross. Did he get fired?" She asked.

"Oh yeah, he's gone," Krista told her. "Let's see, what else can I tell you?" Krista asked herself. She started applying the color to Abby's hair as they talked.

"Oh yeah, I almost forgot. Becky and Jake are getting divorced. Too bad," Krista told her, shaking her head sadly.

"What? Why? Becky and Jake have been together since we were sophomores!" Abby told her.

"I know, right? I guess they are telling people they grew apart. Rumor is it was a wife swap gone wrong," Krista told him.

"Really? Crazy! I wonder if there's any truth to it.

They have two kids together and they've been together so long," Abby said, sad to hear of a couple together so long getting divorced. She wondered if the rumor had any truth to it.

"Yes, it is sad," Krista agreed. "I think that's all the gossip I have today. Been a quiet couple weeks on the gossip front," She told her.

They chatted for several more minutes and then Abby sat back to relax while Krista put the last few foils in her hair. After that was done, she got up and went under the hair dryer for a while and read a magazine while Krista went in the back.

After the foils were done, Krista washed her hair and then they headed back to her station to get her hair cut. Krista worked on it for several minutes, cutting layers in all the right places to make Abby's waves bounce to life.

When her haircut was done, Krista styled Abby's hair, scrunching it up to make the waves take shape. Abby was very happy with the results, as she usually was.

"Well, it was great to see you again. See you next time," Abby told Krista.

"Sounds good. I want to hear all about your date with Max. Good luck, Abby. You deserve happiness!" Krista told her.

"Get some sleep tonight, Krista," Abby told her, knowing it wasn't Krista who could control whether or not she got any sleep.

"I wish it were that easy!" Krista said and then hugged her friend goodbye.

❤ ❤ ❤

Saturday finally came and Abby spent the first part of the day inside, whipping up a new dessert she'd thought up, and then the rest of the day outside doing yard work.

The day was beautiful and she was happy to be out in the sunshine. She mowed the lawn, weeded her vegetable and flower gardens, and then sat back and relaxed in her hammock the rest of the afternoon. She fell asleep at 3:00 pm being so relaxed.

At 5:00 pm, she woke up with a start and panicked after looking at her watch. He'd be there in one hour and she still had to shower and get ready!

She ran inside, turned on the shower, and went to pick out an outfit while the water warmed up.

She used her favorite soap, which smelled like freshly picked lilacs. She had found it at the Minneapolis farmers market and continued to buy it from the seller's website. Serenade Products was the best, with hand-made, all-natural merchandise. Her second favorite was the lilac soy candles, which she also had burning during her shower.

Afterward, she took extra care with her hair, which she scrunched up just like Krista had done at the salon, and was happy her hair looked so good. Her curls bounced to life and the light blonde highlights looked incredible against her tanned skin.

She then applied her makeup, making her eyes look even bigger than normal. She had to admit she looked pretty good and hoped the extra attention made Max's eyes pop out of his head!

She wasn't trying to impress him. Okay, that was a lie. She was trying to make him look twice. It just felt good that after all of the years of her having a crush on him as a boy, he was paying a little attention to her.

She got ready in the nick of time, quickly putting on her favorite pair of jeans and a pretty new teal tank top that showed off her summer tan and toned shoulders. She grabbed a thin white sweater and she was all set with 5 minutes to spare to allow her to quickly paint her toenails bright pink. She had some new strappy white sandals that made her feet look smaller than the size 9 she was.

As she painted her toenails, she started getting nervous. What if he didn't show up, like that time when she was a kid?

No sooner had she started thinking all of these thoughts than the doorbell rang. Abby rolled her eyes at her insecurity.

On her way to answer the door, she popped into the bathroom one last time and applied some lip gloss. She was happy with the results and hoped she got the look from Max she was going for.

She took a deep breath and opened the door. There, stood Max with a bunch of the most beautiful summer flowers she'd ever seen; lilies, roses, and daisies all in a pretty pink vase.

Max was almost speechless. He couldn't believe how incredibly beautiful she was.

He opened his mouth and wished he hadn't.

"Ah, um, well, I mean, good evening, Abby. These are for you." Max thrust them towards her, feeling the blush creep up his neck and into his face.

"Max, these are beautiful. Thank you." Abby took the flowers, slipped off her sandals, and brought them into the kitchen. She set them in the middle of the kitchen table. She looked at them longer than necessary to hide her smile. She had rendered him speechless! She did a little happy dance in her head and then took a deep breath to pull herself together.

That was the exact reaction she had been hoping to see on Max's face so her effort had been worth it. She finally forced herself to quit grinning and turned back towards Max, who was still standing in the same spot.

"Are you ready to go?" Abby asked. She couldn't believe this. It was almost like one of the imaginary reunions she'd dreamed of for years after Max had left.

Max finally found his wits and said, "Yes. Let's go." Max took her arm and escorted her out to his car.

"You still have your Camaro? I can't believe it!" Abby said to Max.

Max looked at her in surprise. "Yes. I can't believe you remember it."

Abby blushed again, this time remembering how many times she wished she'd be asked to ride in his 1969 cobalt-blue convertible Camaro.

"Did you get it painted or something? Last time I saw it, the car looked a bit rusty," Abby said opening herself up to even more embarrassment for remembering the shape the car used to be in.

Max looked even more surprised. "Yeah, I restored it from the ground up! It took me five years. I completely dismantled the car then I had the body media blasted, did all of the metal work, painted it a custom cobalt blue. I had all of the chrome replayed. I restored the interior, put custom leather seats in. I put in a custom digital instrument panel and a premium sound system. I rebuilt the engine; it's a 600 horsepower big block. I rebuilt the suspension and put in a new 12 bolt posi rear end in it." Max told her, very proud of how his hard work had panned out.

Abby listened to what he was saying and said, "So you did paint it." She was thinking she wasn't sure what a lot of that meant but knew it looked nicer.

"Uh, yeah, I painted it," Max said and laughed. Then, he said, "Shall we get going?"

Abby nodded and smiled. "It looks good."

Max asked her as they walked towards the car, "Do you want me to put the top up?"

"No way! Let me just tie my hair back quickly and I'll be set," Abby replied. She grabbed a binder from her purse and tied her hair back. Although she spent a lot of time on her hair, she had always wanted to ride in his Camaro with the top down and wasn't about to let that opportunity slip by.

"We're off," Max said and backed out of her driveway, happy that she wanted to keep the top down.

They drove through town to a small restaurant called "The Vineyard", which was in Ramsey. They chose a table outside and a waiter came over and took their drink order right away. She ordered a glass of Riesling and he ordered a Bud Lite.

"So do you still play basketball, Abby?" Max asked.

Surprised to know he knew anything about her at all, she answered "Yes, I do. I coach the elementary school girls' basketball team and I love it. They try so hard all season long and every year I'm amazed at how much they improve. The season is starting again next week so I've been trying to prepare for that. I have 13 girls on my team this year," She said proudly.

"Really? That's great. I didn't know you did that. I guess I don't know much about you," Max replied.

"So, what do you do for fun?" Abby asked, smirking because she was thinking he didn't know anything about her at all.

"I like to hike. Being outdoors is what I need after being stuck inside an office all day. Don't get me wrong; I love my job. But I love the outdoors more. I'll have to go find some trails around here. Unless you know of any?" Max looked at Abby, kidding around. He doubted she'd be into hiking.

Abby was surprised to find they had that in common too. "Yes, actually I know all the trails and paths around home. I do a little hiking myself," She replied.

Before Max could reply to that surprising answer, their dinner arrived at the table. The waitress placed their food in front of them and asked if they needed anything else. Both Max and Abby shook their heads no.

Abby and Max had a very nice dinner and almost surprisingly to Abby, conversation flowed well throughout dinner. They chatted easily about college, their careers, and their parents.

Even more surprising, they found they had quite a bit in common. There was only one awkward moment when one of Max's ex-girlfriends from high school stopped by the table. She completely ignored Abby and gushed all over Max.

"Max James? It's me, Tracy Anderson. I haven't seen you in ages! How are you?

You look fantastic!" She got down on one knee so she could stare directly into Max's eyes and gave him a nice view right down her shirt. Abby just rolled her eyes at the girl. She was very pretty and knew it.

Max replied to her, "Yes, I remember you, Tracy. I'm doing well. How are you?"

"I'm great! Recently single, I might add." She gave him a wink and a nudge, still completely ignoring Abby.

Abby just sat there and watched, not exactly knowing what to do. Max looked uncomfortable at first and Abby was just thinking she wanted to see how he handled the situation when he introduced her to Tracy.

"You've met my girlfriend before, haven't you? Abby Simon? She was a few years behind us in school." Max gestured towards Abby and then grabbed her hand, which had just been about to pick up her wine glass.

Abby's hand tingled at his touch, and it almost made her pull her hand back.

Tracy looked over at Abby and looked as if she'd just realized Max wasn't sitting alone at the table. She had a look of utter surprise on her face.

Tracy looked down her nose at Abby, although she wasn't sure how since Abby was higher in the seat than Tracy was squatting on the floor.

"Yeah…nice to meet you." Then, she looked back at Max and said, "Can't say as I remember her. She doesn't look familiar at all." Tracy replied as if she wasn't sitting right there.

Abby replied, "Nice to meet you too, Tracy." Although she remembered Tracy, she almost told her she didn't remember her either, but decided she didn't need to sink to Tracy's level.

"Well, if you'll excuse us, we were just in the middle of a private conversation," Max told Tracy, hinting they wanted to be alone.

"Right," Tracy replied, shocked at being dismissed. "Well, see you later. And call me when things don't work out with Annie, here," She said to Max while nodding her head towards Abby, and then gave him a wink and sauntered away. She had a way of swinging her hips from side to side, which caught the attention of many male customers in the bar.

Abby said under her breath, "It's Abby…", and shook her head.

Surprisingly, when Abby looked back at Max, he wasn't looking at Tracy walking away. Instead, he was looking at Abby with an apologetic look on his face, taking his hand away from hers.

"Well, that was interesting," Max said. "I can honestly say, I only went out with her twice before I realized what she was like, and that was only because she acted like someone else completely on the first date. I'm sorry about that."

Abby just shook her head and took a sip of her wine with her hand still tingling. "It's not your fault, Max, so don't apologize." She couldn't believe someone could act that way. She wasn't even thinking of the fact that Max had called her his girlfriend because she knew he was just trying to tell her he wasn't interested.

"Sorry to have used you as an excuse, but had I not done that, I think she may have grabbed a chair and joined us," Max said, exasperated.

"I would have liked that. In fact, call her back over here and ask her to join us," Abby said to Max, grinning.

"Thanks, but I'll pass on that," Max said, chuckling.

They finished their dinners without any further interruption, and the waitress brought over the bill. Max grabbed it before Abby could even think about it, handing the bill and his card to the waitress before she could leave the table.

"Thanks, Max," Abby told him shyly.

"You're welcome," Max told her and grinned at her with a heart-melting grin. Abby figured if he looked any hotter, she'd self-combust.

Max and Abby finally left the restaurant, carefully avoiding Tracy by going out the side door farthest from her, even though it meant they had to walk around the whole building to get to Max's car.

❦ ❦ ❦

"So, I hope you're up for a concert in the park. It's a great band," Max said to Abby. The park in Anoka had bands play occasionally during the summer and he remembered going as a teenager.

"Sure! I haven't ever actually gone to one, which is odd because they have these concerts every weekend each summer." Abby was always up for trying something new.

Max had brought a blanket and a picnic basket with dessert and wine. They got to the park and chose a secluded spot near the back.

The concert was supposed to start in a few minutes so they quickly got their blanket spread out and the picnic basket unpacked. Max poured Abby a glass of wine and gave her a piece of the cheesecake he had picked up at her shop.

"The wine is very good. Thank you. The cheesecake tastes just like mine! It's really good," Abby said. She took another bite of the delicious cheesecake.

"That's because it is yours," Max told her. "I picked some up yesterday when you weren't there, and asked Madeline what your favorite cheesecake was and asked her to keep it a secret. She recommended the turtle cheesecake."

It was nice to sit here on a beautiful night sipping wine. It was even nicer to be sitting there with Max. Max, who she'd had a crush on for so long, who she never in a million years thought she'd ever be on a date with. She looked up to the stage to watch the people preparing for the concert.

"I'm glad you like it. It's my favorite," Max replied. He looked back at her and since she was looking up at the stage, waiting for the concert to start, he took the opportunity and just stared.

Max wanted to know everything about her, even though he didn't have that desire growing up. He didn't pay her much attention back then. He knew she had a crush on him and if anything, he did everything he could to avoid her. To be fair, she was a few years younger than him, and by the time he left for college at the age of 18, she was only 15 years old and still looked like a little girl.

She certainly didn't look little now.

Max looked away just as Abby glanced over at him. Abby couldn't help but think he was almost too handsome. She thought the date was going very well and she was pleased with his idea of coming to this concert in the park in Anoka. It was a beautiful night and she was enjoying every minute of it.

The band finally started to play and the very first song took her back to high school.

When Abby heard the first few notes of "Faithfully", by Journey, she knew exactly what song it was and closed her eyes.

It brought her back to the Senior prom. It wasn't her prom that she remembered, but was instead Max's. Abby was one of the freshmen who volunteered to help at prom that year.

Fourteen years earlier...

Abby was in charge of taking tickets from people as they entered. She felt so lucky to see everyone who walked in the doors and got to see the girls in their pretty dresses and the guys in their tuxes. It seemed weird to her to see all those hunky guys in tuxedos, but it sure was fun to see the pretty dresses.

Abby looked up from the table, just as the first few notes of Faithfully started, and saw Max entering the front doors with another Senior, Jessica. Abby remembered thinking the girl was the luckiest person in the world and wished she could have been with Max instead.

Max and Jessica had walked up to the table.

"Hi, Abby," Max said to her happily.

"Hi," Abby managed to squeak out.

"Who is this?" Jessica asked him, not at all threatened by the little freshman at the folding table.

At that time, much to her embarrassment, she had braces on her teeth, glasses on her face, and her bangs were teased as high as they would go. Her dress was horribly ugly and unflattering and she wasn't allowed to wear any makeup yet.

Abby just stared at Max and instantly felt her face heat up. He looked so handsome!

"Abby is my neighbor," Max told Jessica, gesturing to Abby while looking at the much more attractive blonde who was wearing a very flattering dress that showed a lot of cleavage. She had her hair in an updo and her makeup looked amazing. She was not wearing braces, although as straight as her teeth were, Abby was sure she had worn them at some point in her life.

"Nice to meet you, Abby. I'm Jessica," She said, looking at Abby. Jessica could sense immediately Abby's fascination with Max and thought it was adorable.

Abby just nodded in awe at the older girl.

"Should we head into the gym?" Max asked Jessica, taking her arm.

"Yes." Jessica replied and then turned to Abby and said, "You have a great night, okay?"

Abby remembered being surprised at Jessica's sincerity that night. Not all seniors in high school were that nice, that was for sure.

Even Abby had to admit she must have looked horrible back then, especially compared to someone like Jessica. Thank God she had grown out of that stage. Although she hated them at the time, the braces on her teeth straightened them well and she was confident when she smiled.

She had gotten LASIK a few years back and had learned not to rat her bangs to make them four inches high.

♥ ♥ ♥

After the song ended, she opened up her eyes and looked over at Max. She wondered if he would remember that night.

"Did the song take you back?" Max asked her, looking over at Abby with a smile on his face.

"Yes, lots of memories. Did it remind you of anything?" She asked him.

He thought for a minute and then said, "High school, I guess," Max told her, shrugging his shoulders.

"That was your Senior prom song. Don't you remember?" Abby told him.

"I don't remember the song so much but I do remember I went with Jessica Anderson," Max told her, laughing.

"Yeah," Abby said, and then quickly recovered and said, "I mean, really?"

"How did you know that was my Senior prom song?" Max asked her, giving her an odd look.

Abby figured if he didn't remember the song, he probably didn't remember her being there, looking the way she did, and she sure as hell wasn't going to remind him.

"Oh, just because I liked that song and I remembered it was the prom song for the year I was a freshman. Girls tend to remember these things," Abby told him, lying to save face.

"I liked that song too, but don't remember it being our prom song," Max replied.

"Whatever happened to Jessica?" Abby asked Max, wondering if they had kept in touch.

"I don't know, exactly. I had heard she went to college, became a nurse, and then got married. That's all I know," Max told her.

"I remember her being very nice," Abby commented.

"Yes, she was one of the nice girls in school. She was always nice to people, no matter who they were. I really liked her for that," Max said.

Abby just nodded in agreement.

When the concert was finally over, they picked up the blanket and picnic basket and walked through the crowd toward Max's car.

"Did you enjoy the music?" Max asked Abby.

"Yes, very much. The latest hits were nice, but I loved the flashbacks. Journey, Prince, Queen, I loved them all," Abby replied. "Did you enjoy it?" She asked Max.

"Yes, I've seen this band before and I like them. And it was definitely a nice night to be outside," Max replied, smiling.

He was trying to get up the nerve to ask her to go hiking in the morning. They got to Max's car and he put the picnic basket in the trunk and opened the door for Abby. She got in and he walked around the back of the car.

"So, do you have plans for tomorrow morning?" He asked Abby as he got into the driver's seat. Abby looked at Max and thought, was he going to ask her out again already?

"Other than sleeping in? Not really. Normally Sundays are a huge baking day for me, but Madeline said she could handle it tomorrow. She had already asked another worker to come in and help her bake so I could take a day off. I love that woman!" Abby said.

"Oh, well she sounds like the perfect employee."

Max replied and continued. "I was wondering if you'd mind showing me those hiking trails. I've been dying to get back to hiking; I haven't been able to since I got here," He said.

Abby wasn't sure if hiking could be considered a second date, but she didn't care. "Sure, I guess I could forego the sleeping in tomorrow. What time do you want to get going in the morning?" She asked.

"How about if I pick you up at 6:00 am?" Max suggested. "We should get going before the afternoon summer heat kicks in.

"Make it 7:00 am and it's a deal," Abby replied, grinning at Max, thinking even 7:00 am would be sleeping in for her since she normally got up by 3:00 am.

By the time they had agreed on when he'd pick her up in the morning, they were pulling into Abby's driveway. Max shut off the car and got out. He was around to her side of the car and opening the door before she'd even had a chance to grab the handle.

Max walked her up to the door and watched her put the key into the lock.

Abby turned to Max and said, "Thank you for a lovely evening. I had a great time. See you in the morning?" Abby said it like a question to confirm.

"Yes, I'll be here at 7:00 am," Max replied. He leaned in and gave her a quick kiss on the cheek.

Abby gave him a little wave and walked inside her house. She leaned up against the door and shut her eyes.

She opened her eyes and saw the beautiful flowers in her kitchen. She was finally able to do that happy dance she had only been able to do in her head earlier.

Abby almost couldn't believe it, but she had just been on a date with Max James and she was seeing him again in the morning.

♥ ♥ ♥

Abby didn't sleep well. She tossed and turned and dreamt that she got up and was ready in the morning but kept waiting for Max who never showed up.

A bolt of thunder woke her up and she looked over at the clock which read 2:13 am. Why did she have to be so insecure? It was Max who had asked her out for last night's date and it was Max who asked her to show him some hiking trails today. For once, he was the one who was making the effort.

Abby found herself in bed at 2:30 am, listening to the summer storm and wondering if Max remembered her as that tall, lanky girl who at 15 was still flat as a board.

Abby finally started looking less like a little girl and more like her teenage friends the summer she turned 16. She grew boobs almost overnight and made the change from a child to a young woman that summer. She often wished Max was still around at that time because she was convinced, he'd have finally noticed her that summer.

By the time Abby started her senior year, she was asked out a lot. She dated different guys, but she was never really interested in any of them.

Mostly she hung out with friends, especially her best friend Colleen. They were so much alike; they loved to read, they were both very good in school and they were inseparable from the time they met at the age of 9. The two told each other everything. That's why she had the sudden urge to call Colleen and fill her in on the date.

Abby reached over and grabbed the phone. She'd understand why she just had to call her this late. Abby knew Colleen's fiancé would be at work since he worked the night shift at the hospital. They were getting married the following month and Abby was throwing her bachelorette party the following weekend.

The phone rang three times and then a very sleepy Colleen answered the phone. "This better be good," She said into the phone.

"Hey, Col. Were you sleeping?" Abby asked, knowing full well she was.

"No, Abby, I was cleaning the house. What's wrong?" She asked, and although she was sleepy, she could still crank out the sarcasm.

Abby told Colleen about the date. She told her about their hiking trip planned for the following morning, too.

"I haven't been able to sleep because I'm worried about tomorrow, or rather this morning. I'm not sure if this is a second date or what. And now I'm worried because my mind has brought me back to when I was a kid with a crush. What if he doesn't show up? What if I'm making more out of this than he is and I have the wrong impression of his attention towards me?" All of her fears just spewed out.

"Oh, Abby." Colleen sounded a little more awake now. "You are a successful, beautiful woman. Did you ever think that maybe he finally just realized what a catch you are? You're a different person than you were back then. You were great back then too, don't get me wrong, but you've grown up and done well for yourself," Colleen said. She always knew the right thing to say. "And I know dating after Adam has been hard, but maybe this one is finally going to work out for you."

"I don't know. I guess we'll see," Abby said, and then said in an excited voice that reminded her of their phone conversations in high school, "I cannot believe we're talking about Max James right now!"

"Neither can I, honestly, but I think it's great. What a hottie! Now get some sleep and I'll see you tomorrow. I need full details at lunch." Colleen told her.

"Okay. Love you," Abby said and hung up the phone.

Colleen always made her feel better. She fell asleep within about 2 minutes and didn't wake up again until the alarm went off at 6:30 am.

Chapter 5

Another No-Show?

$\mathcal{M}$ax didn't sleep well. He thought their date had gone well, at least well enough that she agreed to go hiking with him that morning. At 5:15 am he finally decided to get out of bed and take a shower. He'd given up on falling back to sleep and decided to take an extra-long one.

He finally got out of the shower and got dressed.

He didn't bother to shave for their hike but put on an extra dose of deodorant and a little cologne. As he was putting on his watch, he looked at the time.

"What the hell?" He asked out loud. He looked over at the clock by his bedside table, which still displayed 5:15 am, but at that time noticed it was blinking. What the hell had happened to his clock?

"Oh CRAP!" Max said, and then grabbed his keys and raced out the door.

His watch showed 7:20 am. He wondered what Abby would say as he walked swiftly towards his car.

♥ ♥ ♥

Abby was starting to get nervous. It was 7:20 am and Max hadn't shown up or called. Where the hell was he? She tried not to get too uptight while she waited. She had another cup of coffee and checked her hair and makeup, which of course she hadn't done much with because they were going hiking.

She checked her outfit and then put her hiking boots by the door. She arranged the flowers Max gave her the night before and then got out of the vacuum and started with the kitchen. By the time she got to the living room, it was 7:30 am, and still no sign of Max.

She had just started cleaning the guest bathroom when the doorbell rang. So, he decided to show up after all.

She managed to open the door with a smile on her face and there he stood, out of breath.

"I'm so sorry, Abby! You wouldn't believe what I went through to get here this morning!"

He told her.

"Try me," She said, leaning against the doorway, with a smirk on her face. She wanted to know what excuses he'd come up with. Plus, she just wanted to sit there at stare at him. He was breathing hard and he hadn't shaved so he had the stubble on his face that she loved on a man. His face was flushed from obviously running up to the door and his blue eyes were shining bright. It was only 7:40 in the morning, but he looked like a GQ model, ready to go out on the town. It made her weak at the knees.

"Well, when I looked at the clock, it said 5:15 am. After my shower, it still said 5:15 am.

We had a power outage last night and I have no idea why." He started.

"Um, couldn't have anything to do with the huge thunderstorm we had, could it?" Abby asked him, laughing.

"Thunderstorm?" Max asked in surprise. He thought he hadn't slept well but managed to sleep right through a thunderstorm.

Abby just nodded her head and laughed.

"I guess. Anyway, then my Camaro wouldn't start. I left the lights on and it drained the battery. I tried to charge it but it was taking too long with my dad's ancient charger. I decided to take my dad's car so I had to wake him up and convince him to let me take it. Then, driving over here, there was an accident that held up Highway 101. I finally decided to try back roads and I was going fine until I was stopped by the longest train in the history of trains," Max told her all of this, almost as exasperated just retelling the frustrating experience he'd had that morning trying to get there.

"Hmm, that's quite a story. That's ok. I got some of my cleaning done. Nothing like a good cleaning to get warmed up for a hike!" she told him.

"Sorry, Abby. Anyway, are you ready?" He asked her, who looked bright and cheery that morning. It was a welcome sight.

Abby raised her eyebrow and said sarcastically, "No, I'm not quite ready yet." Then she laughed at the look on his face and said, "Let's go."

Abby grabbed her water bottle, handed one to Max, grabbed her keys, locked the front door, and headed down the driveway. Max headed towards his dad's car and she shook her head no. "The best trail is only a few blocks from here. We'll walk. Even though I'm all warmed up, that'll warm you up." She couldn't help but put in one last dig about him being late.

"Fine, I get it; I was late! Sorry," He said, laughing, but then tried to take it to his advantage. "To make it up to you, can I take you out to lunch after we get back?" He asked.

Abby laughed. "You don't have to make it up to me."

"I want to," He replied, thinking he liked her laugh.

"Thank you, but I'm supposed to have lunch with a friend, anyway," She said.

"Anyone I know?" Max asked, raising his eyebrow. Okay, he wanted to ask if this friend was male or female and if the male wanted to know how serious it was. He was already very interested in Abby and wondered if he had any competition.

"Colleen. She's getting married next month and I'm planning her bachelorette party. We're having lunch to talk about the details. She may get upset if I break our date," Abby told him, knowing all too well that Colleen would have no problem with her breaking their lunch plans for more time with Max.

"Oh. Well, I understand," Max replied. They were walking up a hill towards the hiking trail entrance and they were just about there.

Abby kept walking in silence, a little disappointed he gave up so quickly on lunch.

"Maybe dinner this week would work better. What night would work for you?" Max asked hopefully.

"I'll have to look at my calendar when we get back. I know I have a few nights booked this week already. I have our first basketball practice on Thursday night and then I have the bachelorette party and we'll be gone all weekend," Abby told Max as they walked up to the hiking trail entrance.

Max was disappointed. She'd be gone the following weekend. And it sounded like she was busy all week.

"Well, are you ready for some hiking, Max? This is my favorite trail. It has a few rough spots but mostly it's pretty smooth and it leads up to the prettiest view in the whole town. Do you think you can keep up?" She asked in a challenge.

"Oh, I can keep up. Lead the way!" Max replied.

They started walking in silence which allowed him to think about the last few crazy weeks. Max's mother had a stroke and ended up in the hospital. He realized his parents needed his help, so he asked for a transfer at work and then he moved in with his parents. This all led up to the best part which was running into this amazing woman. He wondered what she thought of him.

As they climbed, he had the fortunate view of looking at her very toned backside. She was very fit and had a great body, butt included. He was staring at it when she stopped suddenly and said she needed a water break. He just about bowled right into her but stopped himself just in time. His face turned bright red from thinking about what had almost happened.

They were both breathing heavily as they chugged down some water. He tried not to look at her chest and she tried not to look at his bulging arms.

They took a few minutes to catch their breath and then started back up.

"We have about 20 minutes before we'll make it to the end of the trail. Can you make it?" Abby teased him.

"Yeah, I think I can manage," Max responded, again looking at her butt.

He had never been into hiking when he lived there as a kid. He started hiking in college with some buddies he met and was hooked ever since. It was a fantastic exercise that allowed you to be outside enjoying the day rather than stuck in some sweaty gym with tons of other people all using machines. The gym worked in the winter, but he preferred enjoying the outside whenever possible.

Twenty minutes later, she stopped him again and told him to close his eyes. She took his hand and almost snatched it back again from the instant spark that went all the way to her toes. She sat there for a moment, trying to recover, while still holding onto Max's hand.

Max felt a jolt run through him the second Abby grabbed his hand. He vowed not to let go of her hand until they were heading back down.

Abby shook her head to clear the crazy thoughts she was starting to have and opened up her eyes and looked at Max. With his eyes closed, she could see how long his dark lashes were and got a very good look at his handsome face.

Abby finally took a breath and then led him up a few more steps. They walked a few more feet and then Abby told him to open his eyes. He was still holding her hand when he looked out at the most spectacular view he'd ever seen. He was up high on a hill looking down at the lake he used to fish in as a kid. You could see a trail going around the lake which led out to the park that was right next to it.

The whole time he was taking in the view, Abby was taking in Max's reaction. She had never brought anyone else up there; it was her special place. She hiked up there whenever she needed to get away from everything. It always gave her that feeling, that *this is what life is about* feeling and it helped her put things in perspective. The other thing that gave her that feeling was fishing with her dad, being in the open water staring at the sunrise with a warm cup of coffee in her hands.

"Wow," Max said. He didn't say much else for a few minutes.

Abby remained quiet while he continued to look around him. She was also well aware he was still holding on to her hand and it felt too warm and right to try to take it back from him just yet.

"Wow," Max repeated.

"Yes, you said that," Abby teased. "What do you think of the view?" She asked, turning away from Max and looking out at the open water below them.

Max turned and stared at Abby and said, "I like the view very much," thinking of both the lake below him but mostly of Abby.

A few minutes later, he finally had more to say. "I used to fish in that lake as a kid. Seeing it from this point makes me want to go fishing again. Do you fish?" He asked her, finally taking his eyes away from the view and looking again at Abby.

"I've been known to throw a line out a few times."

She replied. She didn't tell him it was one of her favorite things to do with her dad.

"Care to go fishing with me sometime?" He asked.

"I could probably let you tag along with me and my dad next time we go if you'd like," She told him.

Max smiled at that and nodded his head in silent agreement, thinking she was pulling his leg. She couldn't possibly be into hiking *and* fishing. That would make her too perfect.

"We plan to go Wednesday morning, bright and early. Would that work for you?" She asked.

He gave her a look, wondering if she was serious.

"That would work for me if you think he wouldn't mind another person," Max said.

"I don't think he'll mind," Abby replied. He has a pretty large Warrior Deep V 25-foot fishing boat; it could hold quite a few people comfortably. It was an awesome boat.

Abby finally tried to take her hand away to walk a little closer to the edge but he followed right behind her and gripped her hand tighter. It felt so warm against her cool hand, and she could still feel it in her toes.

She leaned over the rail and looked down towards the lake. She was looking to see if she could spot her dad out there. He often went out there on a Sunday morning to enjoy the fishing by himself. Her dad used to attend church every Sunday but stopped going a couple of years ago, saying he figured he couldn't get any closer to God than in his boat fishing on the crystal-clear lake.

She scanned the lake and spotted him. With her free hand, she pointed to a boat in a little bay of the lake. "See that boat out there, sitting all by itself?" She asked and looked at him.

"Yes," Max replied.

"That's my dad," She said, proudly.

Max looked away from Abby and towards the area, she was pointing to and saw a rather large boat with one person standing there, fishing.

"Really? I almost thought you were just pulling my leg about fishing," Max said, and looked back at her, right into her eyes which were a very pretty green color. She stared back into his eyes until she finally had to look away. She stood up.

"Abby, why are you single?" Max asked her, surprising both of them.

Abby looked at him, laughed, and then shrugged her shoulders thinking, if he only knew. "Why are you?" She asked in return.

Max continued, looking back out at the lake. "I haven't dated anyone since my divorce. A couple of friends tried to set me up but that's about it."

Abby hesitated for a minute but decided to share her recent dating experiences. "Yes, well, blind dates suck. I was on a date a couple of days ago, which didn't go well at all, and the last serious relationship was a year ago with my ex-fiancé," She said. She wasn't sure if she should have opened that can of worms but she figured she might as well get it out on the table now.

"Fiancé?" Max asked, even though he knew a little about what happened from his dad, hoping to hear more from her than he had heard.

"*Ex*-Fiancé, Ex. There's not much to tell," Abby replied and looked toward the lake before continuing. "We dated for a year. He was a nice guy, very handsome, and successful. The day of the wedding, he called it off. He never did tell me why," She said.

"I'm sorry," Max said. He had experienced something similar, although it was after his marriage so he was unfortunate to have divorced in his relationship resume. His wife was cheating on him and had been since before their wedding. "So do you still talk to him?" He asked her.

"I haven't spoken to him in about 8 months," Abby said.

Then, changing the subject, she said, "So, spill. I told you my dark secret. Your turn." Abby prodded.

"Well, I don't think it's a secret that I'm divorced. Rachel and I met in college. We got married and were together for two years. Honestly, I'm really not even sure why she married me in the first place. I wanted kids, but she didn't. I wanted a house in the country, she wanted an apartment in the city. The worst is that she was cheating on me even before the wedding with one of my *friends* from college," Max told her.

Abby was surprised to hear that. Everything she had learned of Max so far surprised her. She had never heard why they divorced. She just stood there looking at him, with an odd look on her face.

"What?" Max asked, noticing the look.

Abby stared at him and finally said, "It's funny, Max. I had this silly crush on you for years, but I didn't realize until this moment that I hardly know you at all."

Max looked at her and said very sincerely, "We can work on changing that."

Abby just gave a small nod in agreement. They were still holding hands when they looked away from each other and just stared out at her dad fishing on the lake. Abby felt one little spark of hope, something she hadn't felt since Adam showed up at her door the day of their wedding.

♥ ♥ ♥

Max and Abby finally decided they better head back down the hill. She still had lunch plans with Colleen so they needed to get back to reality sooner than either of them wanted to.

They made it back to Abby's house in plenty of time for her to make her lunch plans and went inside to get a refill on water.

He saw the flowers sitting on her kitchen table, and it made him smile. He didn't want to take this relationship slowly. Heck, he had every intention of going as fast as she'd let him.

"So, Max, are you brave?" Abby asked him.

"Um, I guess so, why?" Max asked.

"I have a new dessert for you to try. Do you like peaches?" She asked him.

"Sure," He answered.

"I haven't even tried it yet myself. I cooked it up yesterday morning. It's peach crisp, sort of a diet version," She told him.

Max thought diet anything didn't sound all that great, but he'd give it a try anyway.

Abby had put it in her oven in the morning and just kept it on 200 degrees to keep it warm and the top crispy. She pulled it out of the oven and it smelled amazing, he had to admit.

She scooped out two heaping bowls of the peach crisp along with a scoop of reduced-fat ice cream and they sat down at her kitchen bar.

Max took a bite of the dessert and thought he had died and gone to heaven. The lemon dessert was amazing but this was sensational! He couldn't believe it was diet.

"Wow. You sure this is diet?" He asked her, very skeptical.

"Of course. I used a very small amount of organic evaporated cane juice for sweetening and used whole-grain oatmeal with very little brown sugar and cinnamon. I also used less butter and used a little apple sauce to mix it all. Very simple changes that lower the fat and calories and make it a little better for you," She replied.

He hadn't understood anything she had just told him; he just understood it tasted really good. "So, it's diet then?" He asked, laughing.

She laughed. "I wanted to get something on the menu that tasted great but wouldn't make people, especially women, feel so guilty about getting dessert," She told him.

"Couldn't agree more," He told her. "But women worry about that sort of stuff and shouldn't."

She stared at him for a minute with that comment, eating the peach crisp. Was he serious?

"So, this gets your approval?" She asked him, although she thought she already knew the answer.

"Definitely! I'd order this for sure," He told her.

He finished his sample and then said, "Well, I better let you get ready for your lunch plans with your friend. I'll give you a call tomorrow so we can talk about the fishing trip Wednesday morning. I'll also understand if your dad doesn't want a tag-along," Max told her, as he walked toward her front door.

Abby followed him to the door, wondering if he'd kiss her. "I promise; he won't mind a bit. I'll just make sure he's still on for Wednesday. Usually, we leave around 6:00 am. I'm warning you though, if you're late, we'll leave you behind!" She told him.

Max smiled at her and told her he wouldn't be late. He then leaned in and gave her a quick kiss on the cheek.

She shut the door behind him. She would be late for her lunch with Colleen if she didn't hurry up, but she couldn't help it. She couldn't believe what had happened over the last few days. A week ago, she wouldn't have believed someone if they told her she'd go on a date with Max James.

She promised herself she would take it slowly, although she didn't want to. It was funny to her that she thought she was in love with him as a kid. Now, as an adult, her feelings were very different.

Her heart was beginning to open to a new relationship for the first time in a year, but it scared her.

Chapter 6

Best Friends Forever

"Spill," Colleen said as soon as Abby arrived for lunch, 10 minutes late.

"Well, hi there, how are you, Abby? I'm doing fine, Colleen, thanks for asking," Abby said to Colleen.

"Oh, you stop it now. You're late to our lunch and I know you were with Mr. Crush so you don't get to stall," Colleen told her, eyes shining bright with excitement. Colleen's short brown hair was tied back in a short pony tail, and she was wearing yoga pants and a t-shirt.

Abby just grinned. "If you must know, I had a lovely time hiking with Max. We got to know each other a little more. The biggest surprise is finding out how much we have in common."

"And?" Colleen prodded. "Are you going to see him again?"

"Yes, Wednesday morning, actually. He wants to go fishing with my dad and me," Abby told her.

"Well, that's not quite what I had in mind, but I guess it'll do," She replied.

Abby finally gave Colleen the details she'd been dying for. She told her all about their date on Saturday night and then Max showing up late Sunday morning for their hike and finally all about the conversation they had about their ex's. Colleen was just as surprised as Abby with all of the things they had in common.

"So, did he kiss you?" Colleen asked her.

"Does a kiss on the cheek count?" Abby asked her friend, sheepishly.

"Again, not what I had in mind, but it'll do for now." Colleen replied. "Can you bring him to the wedding? It may make it easier to handle seeing Adam." She told her friend.

"I thought about that. I haven't talked to Adam in months and I haven't seen him in a year. I'm sure I'll be fine, but I was thinking about asking Max to come with me. Don't you think it's too early to ask for something like that?" Abby asked.

"The wedding is still weeks away. Give it another week or so and see how it's going. If things are going well enough, ask him!" She said. Colleen was always great with the advice.

The two women had a great lunch, talking about their men, the upcoming wedding, Abby's trip to Napa and the bachelorette party the following weekend.

Abby assured Colleen it would be a classy bachelorette party, rather than a raunchy one as some definitely are.

There were 12 women in total going and would all be staying two nights. Abby had booked three hotel rooms so they would all be comfortable. The first night was a low-key, girly night where they'd spend time in the pool and hot tub and have foot massages at the spa in the hotel. The second night was the main event and they'd be going to a comedy club in Minneapolis.

Abby had also done something that would be a surprise to Colleen and couldn't wait to give it to her the following weekend.

First, she gathered up a questionnaire from all of the friends and family who would be coming to the party, along with her mom and dad and finally her fiancé, Tom. The questionnaire was asking how long the person knew Colleen, how they met, their first impression of her, their favorite memory with her and finally the advice they would give the happy couple about to tie the knot. She then took pictures of Colleen, Tom and their family and friends and put them all in hard-cover photo book using Shutterfly.

She had just received the book in the mail and it turned out to be just amazing. Abby was confident Colleen would have to reapply her makeup when she gave it to her because she cried when she read it.

Abby's absolute favorite page in the book was the very last page, which had the questionnaire filled out by Tom and a picture of the two of them, looking happy as can be the day he proposed. To Abby, it was a sign that they were perfect for each other and their marriage would not only happen but would last a lifetime.

After lunch, Colleen and Abby said goodbye. "I'll see you Friday at the hotel! I plan to be there at check-in time to set a few things up in the room," Abby told Colleen.

Colleen replied, "I'll be there around 6:00pm since I couldn't get the day off. I can't wait! See you then."

The two women hugged each other and left.

♥ ♥ ♥

When Abby got to work on Tuesday, Madeline wanted details.

"Well? How'd it go with the neighbor fellow, dear?" Madeline asked her.

"Pretty well, I guess. We went out Saturday night and then went hiking Sunday morning," Abby told her with a smile.

"Oh, great! I had a feeling, dear." Madeline told her.

"Oh, Madeline," Abby said, laughing and shaking her head, "You always have a feeling!"

"Well, I just have a feeling ya will find that special guy very soon." She told her. "So maybe this is your guy."

"Let's not get ahead of ourselves and jinx it, huh?" Abby told her. With her luck when it came to men, she wasn't going to get her hopes up too much. But man was he good looking so she couldn't help hope just a tiny bit.

"Dontcha think that once ya finally find the right guy, your luck will change? In fact, it's not really luck but fate." Madeline said. She was a firm believer in fate and what will be, will be.

CONNIE STEPHANY

"Well, if so, let's hope Mr. Fate comes knockin' on my door pretty soon," Abby said.

"Oh, he will, he will." Madeline assured her. "Maybe he already has."

♥ ♥ ♥

By Wednesday morning, Abby still hadn't heard from Max for fishing, so she was starting to think Mr. Fate forgot to knock on her door yet again.

Abby had been watching out the window for her dad's truck that morning and he pulled up to her driveway.

Abby ran out the door and down the driveway to his truck. She yanked open the passenger door and almost hopped onto Max's lap. She gave a little surprised yell and hopped back down on the ground, looking at him up in shock.

"Oh, I didn't know you were actually coming today," She said to Max and then turned to her dad. "Hi dad!"

"Hi, honey." Her dad replied.

"Good morning, Abby." Max looked down at Abby, staring. He started to make a move to get out of the truck.

Before he could get out, Abby hopped into the back seat of the truck with the cooler she had packed and said, "Let's go!"

Abby sat in the back seat staring at the back of Max's head. She wished she had put on at least a little make-up that morning. Oh well. He could see her in all her glory at that early hour.

Max sat in the front, trying to keep his eyes forward. He was dying to look back at Abby. She looked very pretty, even though he could tell she didn't have her hair or makeup done.

Max hadn't mentioned to Abby that he wanted to make sure her dad didn't mind him tagging along. Max had called him about it the night before. Abby's dad had assured him he was welcome to come along as long as he could bait his own hook and could pull up an anchor once in a while. Max decided to surprise Abby to see her reaction the next morning.

They drove to the boat launch, where Abby and her dad quickly put the boat in the water. Max and Abby's dad parked the truck, and then got out and grabbed their gear, heading toward the boat Abby had docked.

They had already stopped at the bait shop to get the crappie minnows, fatheads and leeches and they hauled it all into the boat.

"Wow, what a great boat, Mr. Simon. Thanks again for letting me tag along today," Max said to her dad.

"Not a problem, Max. Please call me John. Ready to get going?" He asked both of them. Abby's dad expertly backed the large boat out of the small bay.

They sliced through the water at an impressive speed and before they knew it they were stopping at her dad's favorite fishing spot.

Abby's dad stopped the boat and without him asking, Abby grabbed the anchor and let it drop into the water. Max was awed with their silent teamwork.

"Lines in." Her dad told them quietly.

They all had their lines ready by then so they dropped them into the water. No sooner had Abby dropped her line than she felt her first bite. It took only a minute and she pulled up a nice-sized crappie. Max looked at her with wide eyes, obviously very impressed by her fishing skills.

Abby's dad, noticing Max's expression, said proudly, "She's the best."

"I can see that," Max answered.

For two hours, they continued to fish and pulled in plenty of them. She was very glad the fish were really biting because it gave her something to do other than staring at Max the whole time. She had definitely glanced at him several times, but for the most part she had to concentrate on her fishing. She could also sense him looking her way once in a while, and it put a smile on her face.

They were all ready for a snack mid-morning so Abby pulled out the cooler she had packed and spread out the meat, cheese and crackers after handing them each a hand wipe to clean their dirty hands.

She couldn't help herself and teased Max by saying, "Well, if someone had called me to let me know he was coming, I would probably have packed more."

"Quit teasing, Abby. There's plenty here," Her dad scolded her, laughing.

"Well, again, I appreciate you letting me tag along. And thanks, Abby, for the food," Max told her.

"You're welcome. I was just teasing you anyway. I always pack way too much," Abby said.

Shortly after their snack, they pulled up the anchor and headed back in to shore. As Max helped get all of the fishing gear into her dad's truck, her dad snuck in a quick conversation with Abby.

"So, how are you, Abby? He asked her. "Your mom's been worried."

"I'm fine, dad," She answered him. "She worries too much."

"Yes, well, that's mom for you. So, what's going on with Max?" He asked her.

"We're getting to know each other." She told him, not willing to say anything else about it.

"There's nothing wrong with it, I was just wondering. He seems like a nice young man. I always thought so while you were growing up too. I just don't want to see you get your heart broken again." Her dad said, over-protective of her heart since Adam had pummeled it and he'd had to help pick up the pieces.

"I don't think he'll break my heart, dad. Don't worry about me," She told him.

"I always worry, honey," Her dad replied, as they walked up to the truck, where Max was waiting for them.

"Well, don't. I'll be just fine," She tried to assure him.

They had gotten back to the truck so they got in and headed back to town. Her dad dropped her off at her house and she waved goodbye to Max and her dad.

Abby was a little disappointed that her time with Max was already over and they hadn't spoken about when they may see each other again. He knew she'd be busy that coming weekend so maybe that was why. Or, maybe it was a little difficult to talk about when her dad was sitting right there.

She went inside and took a shower, feeling the need to wash the fishy smell from her hair and nails and body. When she got out of the shower, she got dressed into some old sweat pants and comfy shirt and sat down with the book she hadn't been able to finish.

Chapter 7

Bachelorette Party Weekend

The next morning, Max and his dad surprised her at the shop for some breakfast. She didn't have to wonder long about when she'd see him next! She was glad though, because after they had dropped her off, she tortured herself, trying to analyze the last few dates with Max.

On Abby's recommendation, they both chose her peach bread and some freshly brewed coffee. She brought it over to the table, and before she had even left the table, Max was taking his first bite. She started to walk away.

"Oh, wow, Abby, this bread is amazing!" Max said loudly, still chewing. His comment made her turn back towards the table.

"I know. It's my great-grandmother's recipe that was handed down through the generations. It's one of my favorites," Abby told him.

The peach bread was home-made dough rolled up with peach filling and cinnamon. After it was baked it had a powdered sugar icing on top. When the bread was sliced, it had the filling spiraled so you got a little taste of peach and cinnamon in every bite.

Abby turned to George. "Do you like it?"

"I do, but I always like everything you make. Well, except maybe that one time," George said and smiled at her. Max looked over at his dad, embarrassed by his comment. Sometimes the man had no filter!

It didn't seem to offend Abby, though. "I know; that marmalade was a horrible idea!" Abby said, laughing. "At least you tried it before I served it here. That saved my reputation."

"That was the one and only time, Abby. I'd say that's a pretty good track record," George told her. He always knew what to say to make her feel good about herself.

"I'll let you two enjoy your breakfast," Abby said to them, and turned away.

Max was looking exceptionally handsome that morning. He had obviously shaved and looked like his hair was still wet from his morning shower. He was wearing a blue polo shirt that matched the color of his eyes, and designer jeans that hugged his lower half. She did not want to be thinking impure thoughts about him while his dad was sitting right next to him.

The shop got a morning rush and she was busy while George and Max finished their breakfast. She couldn't help but notice Max glance her way a few times, and she was glad she had decided to do her hair and makeup that morning. She didn't always take the time since she would have to get there so early in the morning, but this morning she did for some reason.

When the morning rush was over, she noticed George and Max were getting up to leave.

"Max, I need to use the restroom. I'll be right back." He told his son, even though he didn't need to. He thought maybe he'd give them a few minutes alone.

"Okay, dad. I'll just sit here and bug Abby for a few minutes," Max told him, letting Abby overhear.

"What are you guys up to the rest of the day?" She asked him.

"Getting the house ready for my mom to come home. The doctors think it may be this week. We need to do a little cleaning before that happens," Max told her.

"Good idea. The last thing she'll want is a dirty house to come home to. It's a woman thing," Abby said, impressed that he was willing to get his hands dirty cleaning.

"So, you have Colleen's party this weekend, right?" Max asked her, switching the conversation.

"Yes! Should be fun," Abby said, excited.

"Is it all weekend?" He asked her.

"I'm leaving Friday night and coming home Sunday afternoon." She answered.

"Oh. Well, you girls have fun. Don't let her get too wasted!" Max said. And don't you meet any men, he wanted to say to her, but kept that comment to himself.

"I'll do my best," Abby said, knowing full well they'd probably do their fair share of drinking that night.

By then, George had come out of the bathroom and told Max he was ready to go.

"Did you want to take home a chocolate cherry brownie or a peanut butter bar?" Abby asked, knowing she could always tempt George into something for later.

"Well, if you're going to twist my arm, I suppose I'd better." George said. "I think I'd like the peanut butter bars. I better take two though since Max will see mine and get jealous."

Abby packed up the peanut butter bars for them, Max paid the bill and they left, waving goodbye to Abby.

Abby had to admit she was a little disappointed he hadn't asked her on their next date, but she figured she'd forget about that by the next day when she was on her way to the party weekend.

On Friday, Abby packed for Colleen's bachelorette party weekend as she listened to Prince. She also made really fun cupcakes with little rings and shoe charms as the decorations on top of each one.

Abby said a little prayer in thanks once again for finding Madeline. She could take the weekend off without worrying about the shop while she was gone. For Madeline taking over for the weekend and now for her trip to Napa, Abby had promised her a few days off so Madeline had been off most of that week and had been eager to get back to work. Abby was pretty sure Madeline loved it there almost as much as she did.

Abby could barely contain her excitement. Colleen had worried this would be a painful event for Abby to plan, but she vowed early on she would not let it get her down. This was about Colleen's joyous event, not about the one that didn't happen.

Besides, she was way too busy to let it get to her! She had to remember all of Colleen's gifts, decorations for the retro "Sex and the City" theme and their outfits for their night out. That was Colleen and Abby's favorite for many years and they both owned all seasons.

Abby's outfit included a sexy new hot pink dress, matching clutch purse and of course her one and only pair of Monolo Blahniks. She had spent a fortune on the outfit but thought she deserved it.

Abby was also in charge of getting Colleen's outfit since the theme was a surprise so Abby had bought a second sexy dress, this one in bright blue to match her best friend's eyes, a second matching clutch and second pair of Monolo Blahniks. Her only defense was that she had gotten both pairs of shoes on eBay, paying much less than she would have paid had she purchased the shoes at a department store. Abby couldn't help it; she went all out for her best friend!

The other girls were all in charge of bringing different items for the party. Amy was bringing flowers for all of them to wear in their hair so everyone knew they were together. Cynthia was bringing wine and Samantha was bringing snacks. Erin had volunteered to bring her iPod and speaker for music. Others were bringing odds and ends, all to make it the most memorable bachelorette party Colleen could ever dream of, or at least Abby hoped.

Abby left her house in the early afternoon, to run last-minute errands for the party and to get to the hotel to bring in the load of wine, cupcakes and Colleen's gifts that had fabulous wrapping. All of the other girls got there well before Colleen finally showed up at 6:30pm.

They went out for dinner at the hotel and then decided it was time to open the wine and sit in the huge hot tub and share their favorite memories of Colleen.

They each took turns, starting with Samantha.

"My favorite memory of Colleen was when we 'haired' Charlie's yard." Samantha began and Colleen started laughing immediately.

"What do you mean, 'haired'? Catherine asked her, confused.

"Well, you know how you toilet paper or egg someone's house?" Samantha asked the group. When she got the nods of yes from them, she continued. "Well, Charlie had TP'd and egged our houses several times, all because I had broken up with Charlie. See, we didn't want to spend any money on Charlie because he just wasn't worth the money. After Colleen had gotten her hair cut one night, we came up with a brilliant idea. We waited until the Great Clips had closed that night and went to the dumpster behind the store. We found bags and bags of hair. It was all different kinds; blonde and brunette, curly and straight. It smelled like perm chemicals," She said, laughing.

"Okay, so what did you do with it?" Catherine asked her.

"Well, we drove the bags of hair over to Charlie's house and spread it all over their front lawn. It looked like it had snowed hair," Samantha told everyone. "They had a pretty small lawn so it covered the entire front yard."

Then, Colleen chimed in and said, "But the best part was the next morning when they had discovered their front lawn."

"Hey, I'm telling the story here, Colleen!" Samantha said, laughing. "But she's right. The best part was when Charlie discovered it the next morning. We were camped out in Colleen's car, parked a little ways away, and we watched Charlie and his mom come outside and look around at the yard in disbelief. You could just tell how mad she was."

The whole group started laughing at the story.

"They were never able to prove anything, but they never touched our houses again after that," Colleen said.

"That's a good one," Said Catherine, who then continued to say, "But I have a funny story too…."

After Catherine told her story, the rest of the girls continued to tell stories about Colleen until they were kicked out of the pool room at 1:00am. The girls headed back to the hotel rooms and went to bed, figuring they'd be staying up very late the following evening.

♥ ♥ ♥

Saturday morning, the large group of women went out for breakfast and then made it to the hotel spa right on time. They were pampered with manicures and pedicures and a few of them decided to get their eyebrows waxed, and others to get a facial.

It was relaxing and fun and prepared them for their "Sex and the City" night out.

Later that afternoon, they had Colleen unwrap her gifts. She received gifts that varied from raunchy to sweet to sexy as hell. One gift made the entire group laugh hysterically.

Colleen started to un-wrap a gift that was in a very pretty box. She hadn't seen a card so she wasn't sure who the gift was from. She opened the box and pulled out a very sexy negligee and held it up for everyone to see.

Catherine said, "Oh darn! I think I got you that same thing."

"Really?" Colleen asked, and kept taking things out of the box. There was some perfume, some edible underwear and some love notes. The last item she pulled out of the box was a sock that looked like a frog.

"Um, wait a minute. That looks like all of the stuff I got you!" Catherine said. She had already had a few drinks and hadn't recognized the box she had wrapped it in.

Colleen held up a sock and everyone in the room started laughing.

"Catherine, what am I supposed to do with this?" Colleen asked her, laughing.

Finally, it clicked with Catherine, who started laughing so hard she started crying. She finally stopped laughing enough to say, "Um, I may or may not have wrapped my sock in your gift," She told Colleen, laughing.

"Huh?" Colleen asked her.

"I was wrapping your gift and somehow lost my sock that I was just about to put on. I couldn't find it anywhere! I should have known," Catherine said, still laughing.

"Oh, thank God! I thought at first it was a penis-warmer for Tom… for the life of me I couldn't figure out why you'd give him something like that," Colleen said, laughing.

"Maybe so you could kiss the frog?" Amy asked, and they all started laughing again.

After everyone stopped laughing from the sock mishap and Colleen had returned the sock to it's rightful owner, Colleen un-wrapped the gift from Abby.

She had purposely kept it for last, because Abby thought Colleen would cry for sure. Colleen read through the book Abby had fondly created for Colleen and as she read each page, she'd look up at Abby. She'd sometimes be laughing and often times be crying, but she started to sob when she read the page her fiancé had filled out for her.

"God, I really love him, you know?" Colleen told the group.

"Awwwww" The group of women said collectively.

"Let me see what he wrote!" Catherine said.

One by one, each of the women took turns reading and gushing over what Tom had written to Colleen. It was heart-warming for Abby to know her friend would be so happy with him and that he really was one of the good ones.

Colleen's very last gift from Abby was her sexy outfit, purse and shoes and Colleen shrieked when she saw it. She knew right away the theme they hid so well. They used to watch the show together and would gush over the shoes they swore they'd never be able to afford. Colleen took one look at the shoes and almost fainted.

"Are you nuts? These must have cost you a fortune, Abby!" Colleen said to Abby.

"Nah, it's totally worth the look on your face," Abby replied.

"Let's go get ready now!!! I want to par-tay!" Colleen said, excitedly.

That's all it took for all 12 women to spring up into action, pulling out dresses, shoes, make-up, hair curlers, irons, hair spray and about 20 different kinds of perfume.

♥ ♥ ♥

A couple hours later, everyone was raring to go. They had continued to have glasses of champagne and wine and had some appetizers sent up to the room while they became "Sex and the City" girls, so they were excited to go out on the town!

Abby had arranged for the hotel shuttle to drive them to the city for the next surprise of the night. They needed to get to the comedy club by 8:30pm in order to keep their seats and it took about 10 minutes to get to the city from the hotel so leaving at 8:00pm was plenty of time.

The shuttle ran only until 10:30pm so they'd have to take a few taxis back. As the driver kept driving and it was 8:20pm, they started to realize something was wrong. He told Abby the directions he was given were not correct. Amy quickly got on her phone's GPS and told him how to get to the comedy club. Abby called the club to let them know they were a few minutes away and the person she spoke with told her it wasn't a problem and they'd hold their seats.

Precisely at 8:30pm, the group of 12 "Sex and the City" girls walked into the comedy club, turning several heads. Abby went up to the counter to let them know they were there and had reservations.

The night all of a sudden came to a halt when the very snotty woman behind the desk looked down at her nose at Abby and said in a high and mighty voice, "Your group was late so we gave your tickets away."

Abby just stared at her and said, "You're pulling my leg, right? Look at us! We're here for my best friend's bachelorette party, I ordered these tickets two months ago, I called to let you know we'd be here in a few minutes and now you're telling me you gave our tickets away?" Abby was furious!

The other girls were already in the bar and had started to order drinks, not even aware of a problem brewing.

Abby demanded to talk to the manager, who told her the only thing he could do was to get the group into the second show, three hours later. Abby told him thanks, but no thanks.

Defeated, Abby walked over to the girls, downed the appletini Amy had gotten for her and told everyone the news. "Well, now what?" She turned to Colleen and said, "I'm sorry, Colleen. I wanted everything to be perfect!"

"Oh, honey, don't worry about it! We'll have fun no matter what we do. I appreciate the thought you put into this party," Colleen reassured Abby.

The group of girls sat in the bar for a few minutes, wondering what to do. Amy started searching for bars downtown Minneapolis and came across a piano bar. Abby liked the sound of that and called the hotel and explained what had happened and asked if the shuttle could come back and bring them to the other side of the city where the piano bar was located. The hotel was great and sent the shuttle right away.

When the shuttle got there ten minutes later, the driver felt so bad that he told them he'd be their sober cab and come and pick them up when the night was over. The group of 12 ladies all cheered and told him it wasn't his fault but they surely appreciated it. He had even brought them each a bottle of water for later.

By the time they made it to the piano bar, they had already had quite a few drinks and were feeling pretty happy, despite the change in plans. Sam and Abby went up to the bar to put Colleen's name in the long line of those to be embarrassed on stage.

"Hey ladies! This will be much better than the dumb comedy club, don't you think?" Abby said to everyone. She was finally over her anger at the comedy club and was ready to party!

"I love you, Abby", said Colleen. "I'm having such a great time. You are the best friend a girl could have," Colleen gave Abby a hug.

"I love you too, Colleen", she replied. "I hope you have a great night and remember it forever."

"I'm pretty sure I will," Colleen said, with a huge smile on her face.

A little while later, Colleen's name was called and she got up on stage and had to dance to "I Touch Myself" by the Divinyls. She milked it up so well there were cheers throughout the entire bar, men and women included. She had no bigger cheering section than the 11 other "Sex and the City" gals there in her honor.

Shortly after her amazing performance, they all decided it was time to hit the next bar so they could all dance. They went to a bar just down the street from the piano bar and stayed the rest of the night, dancing, drinking and having a blast.

Abby met quite a few men, some nicer than others and hit it off with one of the nicer ones, named Jason, who was also very good looking. He was hitting on Abby in a big way and it felt good to her.

Abby figured there was no harm in flirting so they danced and talked and got to know each other a little. She was quite tipsy after talking to him for a while, and felt very brave.

"I just want you to know, I think you're super hot," She told Jason. With as many drinks as she had downed, he could have been Frankenstein for all she knew. But he looked pretty damn good through her buzzed eyes. Plus, a couple of the girls she was with agreed that he was pretty hot.

"Well, thanks. You don't look so bad yourself," He told her, smiling.

She looked at Jason, who had dark hair and blue eyes, thinking he looked a little like Max. No wonder she was so attracted to him.

"Should we go dance?" Abby asked him.

Jason just nodded, grabbed her hand and they headed towards the crowded dance floor.

By the end of the night, he had asked for her phone number. Abby gave him her home phone number so she could decide whether or not she wanted to answer in case he did call, not knowing if she'd actually want to talk.

♥ ♥ ♥

On Sunday morning the girls were packing up, getting ready to check out of the hotel rooms. Abby found herself wondering when she might see Max again. She was debating about calling him to see if he could come over for dinner that night.

Before leaving, Colleen addressed the entire group.

"I just want to tell everyone I had the best weekend with my favorite girls and I love you all very much. I couldn't be happier marrying the love of my life, and you ladies gave me the send off I couldn't ever have dreamed of. In a couple weeks, I will get married and it will become the best weekend of my life with my favorite guy, but I will forever remember this weekend. Thank you, all of you, especially my best friend, Abby, who did the most fabulous job of planning this entire weekend," Colleen had tears in her eyes by the time she was done with her little speech.

They had one last group hug with Colleen in the center, and then they all went their separate ways.

Most of them wouldn't see each other again until the wedding.

♥ ♥ ♥

Abby finally decided to look at the voicemails she had received over the weekend. She was really hoping one was Max.

To her surprise and delight, the first message was from Max, asking if she had plans for that night. Smiling, she wondered if he had somehow had read her mind.

The second message was from her mom, wanting to know how the weekend went, hoping she didn't drink too much. Abby rolled her eyes. It was a bachelorette party. Nah, she didn't drink too much.

The third message was a complete surprise. "Abby, it's Adam. Could you give me a call? I hope you're doing well. Talk to you soon." She was not expecting to hear that one and it caught her off guard.

First, Abby sat down and drank a cup of coffee. She took a few deep breaths to calm down. She decided to call Adam back, but not before she called Max and her mom. What could he possibly want?

Abby dialed Max's parents' number and it rang a couple times before Max picked it up. "Hi, Abby," He said.

"Hi, Max," Abby replied. "So, you're message asked about tonight. You still up for it?" She asked him.

"Of course," Max replied. "Are you?"

"Well, actually, I was thinking a night at home sounds better than going out after being gone all weekend. Would you mind terribly if we stayed in tonight? I'll make it up to you by cooking dinner?" Abby asked him.

"That sounds much better than going out. Although, I've been told you're not a very good cook so I guess I'll just have to force it down," He told her, laughing. "Do you want me to bring a movie?" Max asked.

"Sure, a movie would be nice. I have one request though," Abby said. "Please, no scary movies. I hate them and can't sleep afterward for nights! I watched Candyman when I was a kid and sat up all night looking in the mirror wondering if you said his name in your head three times, if that would make him come to life. When I watched Nightmare on Elm Street, I stayed up all night by drinking diet Coke and watching infomercials because I was sure I'd be sucked into Freddie's house," Abby said.

"Okay, no problem. No scary movies tonight. What time do you want me?" Max asked. He agreed not to bring a scary movie tonight but decided to keep the scary movies in mind for another night, thinking maybe it would work in his favor.

Um, now, Abby was thinking, but knew she needed a shower before she wanted him to come over. Instead, she said, "How about 5:30?"

"Okay. See you then," Max said and hung up the phone.

She called her mom back and was sort of relieved to get their voice mail. She left a message and told her she'd call them back on Monday.

Abby was so excited to see Max she forgot about calling Adam.

♥ ♥ ♥

At 5:25pm, Max walked up to the door and rung Abby's doorbell. He had been determined to be on time.

Abby opened the door and smiled at Max. He looked amazing, and she forced herself to take a breath before speaking. "You're early. Are you hungry or something?" Abby said, teasing him.

"Starving," Max replied, although he didn't care so much about dinner as he did about seeing Abby.

She needed to do a little picking up, so didn't have much time to spend on herself. She had showered in record time, letting her blond hair air dry, and putting on only mascara, blush and lip gloss.

"The lasagna should be done. What movie did you bring?" Abby asked as they walked in her house. She was so glad she had home-made lasagna in her freezer from one of her cooking parties. It came in very handy that evening when she had very little time to prepare something and not much food in her house from being gone for the weekend.

"Lasagna? Really? That's one of my favorites," Max replied, clearly impressed. He looked down at the movie and showed it to her. It was a romantic comedy.

Abby had already set the table, set a couple of wine glasses out and lit a candle. The table looked very romantic and cozy and she hoped it wasn't too forward.

"This looks great, Abby. It smells great too," Max said.

Abby served Max a huge piece of lasagna and then served herself a much smaller piece. She took the garlic bread from the oven and poured the red wine. They sat down to dinner and chatted while they ate.

"My mom got home from the hospital on Thursday. My dad is so happy to have her home," Max told Abby.

Abby's face lit up. "I'm glad to hear that! I'm sure he missed her very much. They probably haven't been apart like that since they got married. How is she feeling?" Abby didn't mention that she was also happy because she realized that was probably why she hadn't heard from him before her big weekend.

"My mom is doing much better and the dizzy spells are gone," Max told her. "I think I'll probably stay for a few more weeks and then start looking for a place of my own."

"So you plan to stick around for a while, then, huh?" Abby asked him, glad to have gotten the opportunity. She had been wondering for a while what his long-term plans were but had been scared to hear his answer.

"I'm not going anywhere," Max told her, looking into her eyes.

"Well, I am," Abby said, smiling, taking a sip of her wine.

"Huh?" Max asked.

"My parents surprised me with something a couple weeks ago. They booked a trip for me," Abby said, and then told Max all about the trip they got for her and all of the plans she'd made since finding out about the trip.

She had already booked a couple tours and a hot air balloon ride over Napa Valley, on top of the tours her parents had booked. She also left a lot of time for just relaxing and was looking forward to it.

Max was happy for Abby, although he was a little sad she'd be gone for so long.

He wondered if she'd miss him while she was gone and he decided to see her as much as she'd let him over the next few weeks to make sure of it.

After they finished dinner, they cleaned up the dishes. She had made dessert but they were both too full to eat it and both agreed to wait until after the movie.

They went into Abby's living room and Max was in shock.

Abby's sofa was a leather recliner, which faced the large 60 inch HDTV and the love seat sat off to the side. Max may just have fallen in love at that moment, seeing the huge TV.

Abby sat down on the sofa, wondering where Max might sit. He wasted no time after putting in the movie in her Blue Ray player and sat right next to Abby.

As the previews started playing, he turned towards her and said, "Abby, thank you for cooking dinner. It was delicious."

"You're welcome. I'm glad you were willing to just stay in tonight. After being gone all weekend, I couldn't find the energy to go out again," She said, and looked at him.

Max looked at Abby and again found himself thinking about how beautiful she was. Hell, she was hot.

On impulse, he leaned in and gave her a kiss.

Although the kiss lasted only a few moments, Abby felt it all the way to her toes.

Max and Abby watched the movie, laughing at many of the same parts. At the beginning of the movie, they were close together and a short time later Max put his arm around Abby and she snuggled up against him.

He kissed her several more times during the moving and by the time the movie was over they were making out on the couch, completely oblivious to the credits rolling.

Max finally stopped himself and sat up. He glanced at the TV and noticed the movie was over.

Abby, still catching her breath, turned towards Max and suggested, "Ready for dessert?"

"Hmm, maybe," Max said to her and raised his eyebrow. When Abby looked at him, he leaned in and gave her another kiss, but then quickly got up and pulled her up with him.

"Now?" Abby asked.

"Yup," He told her, nodding his head and smiling.

Abby, while still recovering from the make-out session, took out the raspberry pie she had made with the raspberries from her back yard. It was still a little warm.

She served Max a large piece.

He bit into the pie, thinking he couldn't help but think about Abby and how he was falling hard and fast. Not only was she beautiful, she was really nice, they had a lot in common and she was the best cook he'd ever met.

When his second piece of pie was gone, he helped with the dishes and the got up to leave.

"Hey, I've been looking at maps and found a place I think would be great for hiking. Would you be up for a long hike on Tuesday morning? I know you work Tuesday night so I thought maybe you'd be free?" Max asked, hopefully.

"That sounds great. I can work off some of the calories I consumed this weekend!" Abby replied, happy that he had remembered her work schedule.

"So, did you meet anyone interesting this weekend? Get any dates?" Max teased her.

"Well, actually, at one bar, I met a guy and we actually really hit it off. He was very nice and we danced and he bought me a couple drinks. At the end of the night he asked for my phone number," Abby said to him, wondering what his response would be.

"Oh, is that right? And did you give him your phone number?" Max asked Abby, hoping the answer would be no.

"Yes, I did, actually," Abby replied, letting him sweat a little. Then, noticing Max's smile drop a little, she said, "Don't worry though, he won't call," Abby said.

"If I met you at the bar, I'd call," Max told her.

Just then, the phone rang, and they looked at each other.

"Maybe that's him!" Abby teased and laughed. She debated about answering it and then let the answering machine pick it up and they both listened in complete shock at the voice on the machine.

"Hi Abby, this is Jason. We met the other night at the bar? I was wondering if you'd like to go out sometime. Give me a call back when you get a chance. Hope to hear from you soon. Bye." The low voice left his number and then hung up.

Abby's face became very red as she looked from the answering machine to Max and back to the answering machine.

"Um...," She said. How awkward.

"See? I guess Jason is a smart guy. Told you he'd call," Max told her.

"Oh well. I never thought he'd call or I probably wouldn't have even given him my number," Abby told him. "We talked, danced. That's it," She said, feeling like she owed him an explanation.

"I knew he would. Like I said, if it had been me, I would have called," Max said, giving her the compliment. He was nervous that she'd want to go out with him.

"What should I do now?" Abby asked, not sure if she should call him and let him down or just not respond.

"Well, I guess it all depends on if you want to go out with him," Max replied, giving her an odd look and thinking it was a strange conversation they were having.

Abby waved her hand in the air and gave him a funny look. "I didn't mean it *that* way, Max! I meant from a guy's perspective, would you rather get a call back or just never hear from me?" She asked him.

"Oh," He paused and thought about it. "Well, I guess you could call him and tell him you're seeing someone," He told Abby, with a little hesitation in his voice.

Abby smiled and tipped her head to the side. She knew things were going well; this could be considered their fourth date. "Yeah?" She asked him.

"Hell, yeah," Max replied and then he pulled her to him and kissed Abby again, with a smile on his face.

Abby reached over and pressed the delete button on her answering machine. She then looked back at Max, shyly.

Max's full-blown grin made her weak at the knees, but also gave her confidence for her next question.

"With that settled, I have a question for you," Abby said to Max.

"Okay, shoot," Max replied, now more confident that was behind them.

"My friend, you remember Colleen?" Abby asked, and when Max nodded his head yes, she continued. "Her wedding is in a few weeks. I'm wondering if you would go to the wedding with me," Abby said.

Quickly before he could reply, Abby added "Before you say yes or no, I want you to know I'm her maid of honor, so I'll be busy for a lot of the wedding. And…" Abby stopped, and took a deep breath for courage. "I have to warn you that my ex-fiancé and Colleen's fiancé, Tom, are good friends. So…Adam will be there, too," Abby said. "I understand if you say no; it may be a little awkward."

"Sure, I'd love to go with you," Max replied, happy she had asked him. He wanted to see what kind of guy her ex-fiancé was, although he knew he must be a complete idiot considering he let her go.

Abby's smile lit up her face. She wanted to clap her hands and dance around the room but restrained herself and settled with replying to Max, "Great!"

"If nothing else, it should make for an interesting night." Max commented.

"I just hope it isn't too uncomfortable for any of us," Abby said, a worried frown on her face.

"It will be fine." Max assured her, pulling Abby back in to his arms, putting one of his hands on the back of her neck and bringing her head in for another kiss.

Max and Abby stood kissing at the door for a couple more minutes. It started to get really heated and he found himself backing her against her front door. He let it go on for another minute, but he finally stopped the kiss and took a step back, dazed. He looked her in the eyes, and let his heart settle for a minute.

"Thanks for another nice night, Abby." He told her, his voice husky and very low. "I better get going." He was almost wishing Abby would invite him to stay longer, but didn't want to go too far too fast and mess anything up for them.

"I'll see you later," Abby told him, giving him one last little hug.

After Max left, Abby thought about the night and couldn't have been happier. Not only did Max indicate they were seeing each other, he had agreed to come with her to the wedding.

She hugged herself and danced around like she had wanted to do earlier.

Since she'd finally given in to going out with him, things were happening quickly with Max. It was a little scary, but she really liked him. Not just the silly crush she had as a kid, but *really* liked him. She was getting to know the real him.

She figured having Max with her at the wedding would make it easier for her to see Adam. She hadn't seen him in over a year, and it scared her so much even to think about seeing him again. How did he look? Was he as handsome as ever? What would they say to each other? How the hell was she going to face him that night?

One thing was certain. She was glad Max would be there to support her.

Chapter 8

A Familiar Voice

*O*n Monday night, Abby was just sitting down to relax with a new book when the phone rang.

"Hello," Abby said in a sexy voice, thinking it would be Max confirming their plans for Tuesday morning.

There was a pause on the other end of the phone, and the she heard a voice say softly, "Hi, Abby."

Even after eight months, she hadn't forgotten his voice.

"Hi, Adam," Abby said surprised, changing her voice to her normal one.

"How are you, Abby? It's been a long time," Adam said.

"I'm doing well. And you?" Abby asked. Hearing his voice, many of the old feelings came rushing back, especially the pain. She hadn't forgotten that she had loved him and was devastated after he walked away from her.

"I'm okay," Adam replied.

"Glad to hear that, Adam," Abby told him, recovering from her her wave of emotions. "So, what's up?"

"I called because I wanted to talk to you before we saw each other at the wedding. I don't want things to be awkward between us," Adam told her, not mentioning he remembered well that the last time he saw her was the day they were supposed to have gotten married. He continued, "It's Tom and Colleen's day, you know?"

Abby was a little irritated with him for thinking he'd need to remind her of that, but agreed with him nonetheless.

"I'm well aware their day has nothing to do with us, Adam. I would never do anything to make it less than perfect for my best friend. I was looking at it as we'll just happen to be at the same wedding," Abby replied, trying to keep the irritation out of her voice.

"I just wanted to make sure and I thought talking before the wedding would be a good idea, sort of like breaking the ice." Adam said.

"Yes, I guess you're probably right," Abby conceded.

"I do look forward to seeing you, Abby," Adam said softly.

Abby didn't say anything right away. She felt that familiar twinge of regret and emptiness she had felt when Adam told her he couldn't marry her. It was still hard to take. She wondered if he'd be bringing someone with him to the wedding. She also wondered if he had thought of the possibility she'd be bringing someone.

"Yeah?" Abby asked, not knowing what else to say.

When she didn't say anything else, he said, "Well, I guess I'll let you go. I'll see you at the wedding, Abby."

"Yes, see you soon," Abby replied and hung up the phone as she wondered how he looked. She had heard he'd lost a little weight after he had broken it off. She had lost some herself.

Abby shook her head as if shaking it would make those feelings disappear. She picked up her book and started reading, hoping that would get her mind off the phone call she had just had.

The phone call, she knew, was unfortunately nothing compared to how she would feel when she actually saw him in person for the first time since that fateful morning. She planned to prepare herself in every way possible and she thought having Max there would help, even if just a tiny bit.

❤ ❤ ❤

The next morning, Max came over to pick her up for their hiking "date". The new trail he found was not within walking distance, so they hopped in Max's car for the short drive over to the trails.

They drove in silence at first, as Abby contemplated telling Max that Adam had called. She decided the conversation wasn't exactly profound and she could probably skip telling him.

"Penny for your thoughts," Max said to Abby.

"What? Oh, sorry. I was thinking about the wedding coming up. I'm going shopping with Colleen this weekend for her wedding lingerie; although she got quite a bit at the party the other weekend so I don't think she needs a whole lot.

"Oh. Well that sounds like fun," Max told her, and then quipped, "Is someone taking Tom shopping for tools for their house?" Max asked her, figuring tools were the equivalent.

"Ha ha, Max. That's just a woman's right before getting married. Plus, it's more for the man than the woman, anyway," Abby told him.

"Good point," Max said, laughing. Then, stopped laughing abruptly and cleared his throat when he pictured Abby in some sexy little negligee.

They pulled up to the small parking lot and parked the car. They both grabbed their water bottles, Abby grabbed the little back pack that contained lunch and Max grabbed a larger back pack that had a blanket.

They took off on their hike, enjoying the silence. Max could hear Abby's breathing, which got a little more strained as they hiked up a small hill.

Abby continued walking and decided to break the silence. "I was thinking I'd bring everyone dinner Wednesday night. Do you think your mom would be up to a visit?" Abby asked Max.

"I think she'd love a visit, especially if it means food that doesn't come from a box or a can or being delivered," Max replied. "Plus, she'd love to see you again. Would you be bringing some dessert, too?"

"No dessert. I'm all dessert'd out. Aren't you?" Abby asked Max, teasing.

"Oh, hell no," He told her.

"Any requests?" She asked him, wondering what his favorite may be.

"I don't want to sway a creative genius in any way, but one of my favorites is banana cream pie." He told her, his mouth watering just thinking of it.

"Banana cream?" Abby scrunched up her nose. "Really? Okay, I guess I can do that," Abby told him.

"You don't have to make that one. I was just telling you what I like. My mom likes it too, but she likes just about any dessert." He told her.

"Well, banana cream pie it is, then," Abby replied.

The talk of pie made them hungry for the lunch she had packed.

They hiked a few more minutes and then found a nice clearing in the woods, perfect for a picnic.

Max laid out the blanket while Abby took out lunch. She brought something pretty simple for lunch that day. She packed summer sausage, cheese, crackers and grapes. For dessert, she had decided on couple chocolate chip cookies, made from scratch using her secret brown butter recipe. No one could resist her chocolate chip cookies.

While eating, Max decided to plan for the next date. He figured he wouldn't leave one date without making plans for the next. He wanted to keep things going with Abby.

"So, when are you going shopping?" He asked her.

"Sunday afternoon," Abby replied, remember the conversation she'd had with Colleen, who had told her she wanted to keep Abby's Saturday evening free in case Max wanted to see her that night. Abby smiled at her friend's thoughtfulness.

"So then does that leave your Saturday free?" Max asked her.

"It does," Abby replied.

"Would you feel like taking a drive up to Lake Mille Lacs? I checked into fishing and it sounds like the fish are really biting right now. There's a charter we could take. We bring the beer and snacks, they provide the boat, the guide and the fishing poles. They'll even put on your bait for you," Max told her.

"That sound like fun, Max. Yes, I'd love to go." Abby answered. Fishing was something she truly enjoyed, being brought up near a lake. It was something she really liked doing with her father, since her mom never really cared for fishing.

"Well, great. I'll get the evening charter booked. It starts at 5:00pm so we can go out for dinner first," Max said.

"Okay," Abby replied.

They finished their lunch, talking easily about anything and everything. Abby found spending time with him was never boring and they always found things to talk about.

After lunch, they headed back home because she had to leave for work. As much as she loved her shop, that day she would rather have spent more time with Max.

♥ ♥ ♥

When she got to the shop that day, she told Madeline she could go home since she had been there all day. She didn't feel too terrible for having her work so much, because Madeline always insisted she loved every minute of it. Plus, Abby paid her well.

Before she left, Madeline asked Abby how things were going with Max.

"So, give me details, dear! How are things with that cute neighbor?" She asked.

"Things are going well, I think," Abby told her with a smile. "And he agreed to go to Colleen's wedding with me."

"That's very good to hear. You two will have a good time. And he can keep your mind off Adam that day, not to mention show Adam what he's missin'!" Madeline said.

"Well, let's hope it goes well. I'm dreading the wedding as much as I'm looking forward to it," Abby said, looking worried about it.

"You'll do just fine, dear! He'll take one look 'atcha and regret his decision to walk out on you that day," Madeline predicted.

"Hmm, well I doubt that," Abby said. "Now, get out of here. You're here too much! Go spend some time with your family."

"Okay. Have a nice afternoon. The only things left to bake are the lemon bars and monster cookies," Madeline told her.

"Really? You got the rest done already?" Abby asked, surprised.

Madeline nodded yes, waved and walked out the door.

No sooner had she left when the door opened and walked in Max.

"Hey, there, stranger! What are you doing here?" She asked him. She was surprised he was there, but happy to see him.

117

"I have a sweet tooth and I need to get something to cure it," He told her, but really he just wanted to see her again.

"Well, what do you feel like?" She asked him.

"What do you recommend?" He asked her back.

"I recommend either the seven-layer bars or can't leave alone bars on this fine afternoon. Made fresh just today. Coconut or chocolate, which would you prefer?" She asked.

"How about one of each?" He asked, smiling.

"Good choice," She told him, smiling back.

After she got out his two dessert choices, she put them on two separate plates and sat down with him while he ate them. She also had brought him a cup of coffee and she had one too.

"Well? Which is better?" Abby asked Max after he ate them both.

"I have to say the "can't leave alone" bars are better, although the seven-layer bars came in a very close second!" He replied.

"Good to know," She said.

"So, what time do you close?" He asked her as he was getting up from the table to leave, which was his real reason for stopping in.

"We close tonight at six. Then I have paperwork to do, but I should be out of here and home by 7:00pm or so. Why?" She asked him, following him to the door.

"Just wondering if you'd want some company tonight?" He asked her.

"Sure! What time should I expect you?" She asked.

"How about 7:30pm?" He asked her, hoping that would give her enough time to unwind or whatever she needed to do.

"Sounds good. See you then," Abby said, and since there were no customers in the shop, she stood on her tip-toes and gave him a little kiss on the mouth.

He grinned at her, waved, then left.

As she watched Max walk to his car, she couldn't help but notice a familiar car sitting in the parking lot across the street. She peered at the driver sitting in the front seat and could have sworn it was Adam. She shook her head, thinking her mind was making things up just because she had talked to him after so long.

Chapter 9

Getting to Know You

$\mathcal{I}$n the following couple weeks, Max and Abby spent every spare moment together. It helped to keep Abby's mind from wandering to Adam.

They went on the fishing charter and caught tons of fish, they went to see movies, they went on walks, hikes and he even helped her plan for her trip.

One of his favorite days with Abby was when she came over to his parent's house and relaxed by the pool. She packed a picnic lunch for the whole group, including a tasty new dessert she had created. She had made sandwiches and picked fresh strawberries from her back yard. The dessert was an ice cream cake, perfect for the hot summer day they were outside enjoying.

Sitting by the pool, eyes hidden with his dark sunglasses, Max couldn't help but notice Abby's very toned body in her two piece bikini. She had her hair up in a bun and he was glad he had dark sunglasses because he could pretend to be relaxing on the lounge chair while he was checking her out in her suit.

After dessert, George and Junie went inside telling them it was too hot to stay outside. Max was pretty sure they were just trying to give them some privacy.

Max told Abby his parents were doing well on their own now and he was ready to find his own place.

"Would you mind seeing a couple houses I liked? I wanted to get another opinion," Max told her.

"Sure. I'd love to. I thought you were planning to design your own place though?" She asked him.

"I'm thinking about it. I like looking around at homes for sale to get ideas of what I'd like in my own home. I know I want a modified two-story and I want a huge kitchen with granite countertops and wood floors, but what else? I saw one house that had a four-season porch that I think I'll be adding to the plans. Another had a huge walk-in closet in the master bedroom that had a built-in safe that was hidden behind a closet. I definitely want a huge hot tub in the basement and I want a main-level laundry room. Each house I see I find something else I want so it's been fun looking at houses," Max explained to her.

"It's good you're doing all of that research ahead of time. You'll end up with exactly what you want. Have you looked at any lots yet?" Abby asked him.

"A few," Max replied.

"Well, keep looking until you find the perfect spot," She told him.

Abby was glad to be spending so much time with Max. After she finally let her guard down with him, she realized what a great guy he was. It was good for Abby to stay busy, since it gave her less time to dwell on the upcoming wedding where she'd see Adam.

Max and Abby talked about everything, usually over some new dessert she was trying out, from politics to religion to children and family and everything that was important to them and made them who they were.

It amazed Abby how much they actually had in common. They both wanted children some day, they were both Christian, although neither of them attended church regularly and they both had very similar political views. They did have a few things where they had complete opposite views, but on minor things like which baseball team would win the World Series. Although it made for many good conversations, that wasn't a deal breaker.

She even brought up her desire to adopt some day and he just smiled at her and said he liked the thought of that.

Just about every time they got together, especially when they were at Abby's home, they would end up making out. It had never gone farther than that, although many times they both wished it had.

Things changed between them a few days before the wedding. Max came over for dinner and a movie; they both really enjoyed watching movies so it was something they did often.

After the movie they talked about it. The movie was older, and was called Couples Retreat, starring Vince Vaughn, one of her favorite actors. Vince's character was Abby's favorite, because he played a man completely in love with his wife. The movie made her hopeful, that there really was true love out there.

She was even starting to think of Max in that way, where she could see herself actually loving him and in a relationship with him.

After they agreed Vince's character was the best, Max leaned in to kiss Abby good night. They kissed for a few minutes, and Abby was contemplating asking him to stay that night, but she didn't want to be too forward and scare him off.

Max broke away from the kiss and asked nervously, "Can I tell you something?"

"Okay," Abby said. "What is it?"

"I hope this doesn't freak you out," Max said, and then paused.

"What?" Abby asked, worried about the look on his face.

"Abby, I'm falling in love with you," Max told her, nervously.

Abby was shocked. They had only been dating about a month and a half. "Oh," She said.

"Oh? What does that mean?" Max repeated, his face falling just slightly but enough for her to see that he was disappointed in her reaction.

Abby looked at him, right in the eyes, and gave him an ear-slitting grin. "Well, about two minutes ago, I was thinking that it would scare you to know that I was starting to have very strong feelings for you. I'm pretty sure I love you, Max. But I figured it was way too early to say anything to you," Abby said, laughing, and pulling him to her again.

"Oh," Max said, relieved. He was so happy he grinned and then leaned back in and kissed her.

Several minutes later, Max stood up and helped Abby up off the couch, and he asked her, "Do you want me to go?"

Abby shook her head, and said "No, I don't. Stay." Then she grabbed Max's hand and then led him to her bedroom.

♥ ♥ ♥

The next morning, Abby woke up to sounds in the kitchen and the smell of freshly brewed coffee.

She got up, put on a robe, brushed her hair and teeth and then headed down the hall into her kitchen. What she saw made her come to a screeching halt. She found Max in his boxers and a bare chest, making breakfast, sipping on a cup of coffee.

Max turned and gave her a huge grin and she just about fainted. Damn, did he look good in her kitchen! She could definitely get used to this.

Abby was tempted to run over to Max and attack him, but settled for walking quietly up to him and hugging him from behind.

Max turned around in her arms and hugged Abby, and said, "Good morning. I hope you don't mind me digging in your kitchen for food."

"Are you kidding? This is great!" Abby replied, kissing him loudly on the mouth.

Abby grabbed a coffee mug and creamer from the fridge and poured herself a huge cup of steaming hot coffee. She then sat down at the table and just watched Max making breakfast in her kitchen.

After breakfast, they went back to Abby's room to find the clothes Max had left behind and she decided to give him a little thank you kiss for breakfast.

"Hey," She said to Max, giving him a come-here motion with her finger.

He turned to her, said "Hey, yourself.", and quickly walked towards her, kissing her with a smile on his face.

The kiss turned into a little something more and they didn't make it out of the bedroom for another hour.

Chapter 10

A Blast from the Past

The day of the wedding had arrived. Abby was nervous, but not as nervous had she been going alone. Her parents were going to meet her at the church and they were going to bring Max with them since she needed to be there much earlier than they did.

Abby got all of her stuff together, and headed over to pick up Colleen. They were heading out to get their hair done and then they were going straight to the church since the wedding was at 2:00 o'clock in the afternoon.

Abby felt somewhat relieved that it was a little different than her day had been, but it didn't stop the flashes of memories that continued to creep into her head. She ignored the memories and pretended nothing was bothering her.

She and Colleen got ready, and Colleen looked amazing in her dress. At 1:50pm, Colleen's dad came in to sit with her since he'd be walking her down the isle. He had a hard time keeping his eyes dry and Abby came to the rescue with tissues she had brought with in her purse.

Precisely at 2:00pm, Abby was walking down the isle with Tom's brother, Alex. Colleen and Tom wanted only a maid of honor and best man so it was a small wedding party. Then, the entire church stood up to watch Colleen walk down with her dad to her awaiting groom, who looked to be the happiest man she'd ever seen. That sent warm shivers down her spine, to think how lucky her friend was to have a man like Tom.

Abby kept her eyes on Colleen for most of the wedding, but quickly scanned the crowd for her parents and Max. Before she saw them, she happened to catch Adam's eye.

She paused for a minute, wondering what Adam was thinking, but then kept looking for Max, who she knew would give her comfort.

She found Max just a second later, and he was looking right at her. He gave her a very warm smile and mouthed "you look beautiful". Abby just smiled back at him, thinking that was exactly what she needed.

For the remainder of the ceremony, she looked at both Colleen and Tom and didn't look through the crowd again, so she completely missed the two sets of eyes that were glued to her.

Max was watching Abby, thinking he should be struck down where he stood for even thinking it but she was prettier than the bride. He was also wondering where Adam was and wondered if he saw her the way Max did. He couldn't help but contemplate and almost worry whether Adam would take one look at her and want her back. Was Abby over him?

Adam was watching Abby, thinking she was more beautiful than he ever remembered. Many times since the day he broke off their wedding he regretted the decision he had made. For the past year, he had done everything he could to convince himself he had done the right thing, but he never really did believe it.

The day of the wedding, Adam didn't see any other choice. But since that day he was able to see more clearly and seeing her again, he regretted it to his core. He knew then he could still have married Abby that day. He could have told her everything, shortly after the wedding and she would have understood and would have forgiven him. It just didn't seem like the right thing to do so he ended it.

Even after the wedding he tried telling her multiple times and had finally gotten the nerve when she had asked him to stop calling her. It had hit him like a ton of bricks that she was trying to get on with her life and that was when the real regret settled.

In the eight months that followed, he had thought about Abby often and picked up the phone dozens of times but never actually called. He tried to respect her wishes in that regard.

He got into the habit of driving by her shop and would sometimes sit in the parking lot across the street, watching her serve customers. A couple times he thought she saw him, but she turned away without acknowledging him. She deserved to get on with her life, even if he was miserable.

As Adam sat on the church bench, he started to think maybe this wedding would be the perfect opportunity to renew the relationship. He knew he'd have to tell her everything right away, but first he had to gain a little trust back, and he'd work on that starting that day.

"Adam, who are you looking at?" whispered his sister, Amanda.

"The bride, of course. Tom's a lucky fellow," Adam replied to her in a whisper.

"Oh. It almost seemed like you were looking at Abby," Amanda replied suggestively, knowing full well he was. "Don't open that can of worms again. You broke her heart and she doesn't need you to break it again."

Adam didn't respond.

♥ ♥ ♥

The beautiful wedding ended, and the happy couple went off in a limo to the reception, where all of their guests awaited their arrival. Abby kept thinking how wonderful her friend's wedding had been, but the fun part was just about to start.

She didn't want the reception to go fast, but she was looking forward to spending the night with Max in the hotel room they rented together. Plus, she wanted to get her meeting with Adam over, because she knew they'd eventually run into each other at the reception.

After dinner, the DJ set up and started playing some music. After the customary wedding dances were over, the DJ started playing some fun, dancing music. She and Max and some other friends started dancing and had quite a bit of fun dancing to the usual wedding songs, like the YMCA, the chicken dance and the Hokey Pokey.

After dancing to several songs, Abby needed water.

"Max, I'm heading up to the bar to get some water. I'll be back in a bit," Abby told him.

"I can get it for you," Max told her. He was a little nervous about leaving her alone in case Adam might try to talk to her.

"Thank you, but no, I need a quick break," Abby said, and then started walking towards the bar.

♥ ♥ ♥

Abby grabbed a water bottle from the bartender and then she heard the voice she had dreaded hearing all evening.

"Hello, Abby." Adam said, voice low, almost a whisper. He then said, "You look amazing."

Abby closed her eyes, said a little prayer for strength, and then turned around, sipping on her water. "Hello, Adam." Damn it, he looked really good. Why the hell couldn't he have gone bald or something? Nope, he looked amazing, his brown eyes bright and full of life. His hair was styled a little differently and he had grown a goatee, and it looked extremely hot on him.

She turned back towards the bartender and said, "Give me a shot of Cuervo, would you?"

The bartender raised an eyebrow and said, "Certainly. Lemon and salt with that?"

"Yes, please," She replied. She watched him pour the drink and no sooner had he put it down had she downed it, first licking the salt and then sucking on the lemon after the shot.

"Another." She told him.

"Yes, ma'am." The bartender replied, and set her up again.

She downed that one too, and then felt better.

"Whoa, Abby. Slow down," Adam said to her in surprise.

She turned back to Adam, who had watched Abby down the shot with interest. Maybe she wasn't over him yet. Maybe he had a chance.

"Don't worry about me," She replied, fire in her eyes.

"It's been a very long time, Abby. How have you been?" Adam asked her.

"Yes, it's been over a year since I saw you last." She couldn't help but dig the knife just a tiny bit. "I'm doing fine, Adam. You?" Abby asked in return. She noticed he did indeed look a little thinner, but he still was handsome as ever. She felt the familiar pain in her chest.

"I'm ok, Abby. I was hoping to get a chance to talk to you tonight," Adam told her, ignoring her first comment because they both were painfully aware of the last time they saw each other.

"It was inevitable, I suppose," Abby replied, not taking the bait as he'd hoped. But, he was prepared for that too. He decided to just try with the mistake angle and see where it got him.

"Abby, I made a huge mistake," Adam told her, just getting it out there right away. He had made several mistakes, really, he thought. But, he'd start with the biggest.

Abby turned towards Adam, eyes wide. "What?" She asked, utterly shocked to hear those words come out of his mouth.

"I made the biggest mistake of my life that day, walking out on you," Adam told her, wondering if she'd believe him.

"When did you come to this realization, Adam?" Abby asked him, her heart doing a flip-flop.

"I'm going to be honest with you. The very last time we talked on the phone, when you asked me to stop calling you, it was like a slap in the face. Even before that, I was still trying to convince myself I had done the right thing. When you finally ended it, I knew I had made the biggest mistake of my life and I loved you with all my heart," Adam told her. He meant everything he had said and like the day he left, his eyes filled with tears.

Abby saw the tears and it was hard not to feel bad for him. She could tell he was telling her the truth.

She said, "God, Adam! Don't forget, you ended it, not me. And you never even told me why."

"Believe me, Abby, I know that. I'm reminded of that every morning when I wake up and see your beautiful face in the picture beside my bed. I see you smiling at me each morning," Adam said.

Abby knew exactly what picture he meant. It was their engagement picture and one of her favorites at the time. "I look at that picture and think what a fool I was."

"If that's true, Adam, why didn't you call me, or come and see me? Why did you just let me go?" Abby asked.

"I picked up the phone dozens of times, Abby, but I never called because was afraid you'd tell me to get lost. I was going to just try to get over you and let you get on with your life like you asked. But I can't get on with mine. I love you more today than I did when I asked you to be my wife. I would marry you on the spot, if I could," Adam told her.

Abby looked at him and wondered if he'd tell her why he left. It all was very confusing for her.

"I'm not really sure what to say, Adam. You hurt me, more than anyone has ever hurt me in my life. I'm not sure I can ever forgive you for that. You walked out on me on our wedding day, leaving me to cancel the entire event and have to face people by myself. You broke my heart right in two and it's finally now just starting to heal. What do you expect, Adam? Do you think I'll just take you back? After all this time?" Abby asked him.

"No." Adam sighed, shaking his head. "No, I don't expect you to simply take me back," He replied gently. "I'm just hoping you'll consider seeing me again to see if you could ever possibly forgive me." Adam pleaded with her.

By then, Max was wondering what was holding Abby up and started walking over to the bar. Abby noticed him coming.

She turned to Adam and said, "Adam, I'm seeing someone and he's on his way over now. I know this conversation isn't over, but I'd rather it be private. You still owe me an explanation for what happened."

"Ok, as long as you're saying we can discuss it later." Adam said to her, hopefully. Abby simply nodded her head once in agreement.

Adam didn't realize she was seeing anyone. It shocked him, actually, that she was seeing someone. He realized it was dumb not to have thought of that as a possibility.

Max got over there a few seconds later and put his hand on her back. "Hi. You ok?" He asked her.

Abby smiled, thinking how sweet of him, he was trying to protect her.

"I'm doing fine. Max, I'd like you to meet Adam. Adam, Max." How awkward it was for her to introduce the man she was seeing to the man she almost married.

"Nice to meet you, Max," Adam said, cordially. He stuck out his hand, and Max shook it firmly.

"Oh, Adam," Max said. "I was just getting thirsty."

Adam wasn't dumb. He knew Max was coming over here to show Adam he had a claim on Abby.

"Let me buy you one, Max. What would you like?" Adam asked him.

"Just water for now, thanks," Max replied, thinking he'd be dammed if he'd let Adam buy him a drink.

"Okay. Well, I better get going." Adam said to the two of them. He then turned to Abby and said, "We'll talk again soon." He then walked away.

"Are you ok, Abby?" Max asked right after Adam left.

"Yes, I'm fine," Abby told him, not saying anything else.

"You two looked to be in deep conversation," Max said, uneasy.

"Yes. I'll explain later," Abby told him and looked at him. He looked worried. "I just don't want to get into it here at the wedding," She said gently.

"Sure, I understand completely," Max said, trying to be supportive, but couldn't help a sinking feeling he had in the pit of his stomach

Just then, a slow song came on and Abby decided it was just what they needed. Abby turned to Max, snuggled right up to him and whispered in his ear in a very sexy voice, "Max, will you dance with me?"

Abby's warm breath hit his neck, instantly turning him on and making him want to leave the party to go to their hotel room.

Instead, Max controlled himself, smiled, and said, "I never thought you'd ask."

Max and Abby made their way to the dance floor and danced to the next three songs together, all of which were slow songs. Max softly stroked Abby's neck, sending shivers down her spine.

He was trying to give her a taste of her own medicine and he couldn't help but notice it had worked. She had snuggled up closer to him while they continued to sway to the slow music.

After the slow songs ended, Max and Abby went and sat down at the table together. Neither of them noticed the set of eyes staring.

Adam was watching Max, wondering what to do about him. He wouldn't mind getting a chance to talk to him alone. He could see that Max would be some definite competition. Why the hell hadn't he even thought of the possibility that Abby would be seeing someone? He looked over at Abby and thought she looked happy with the guy, but that sure wasn't going to stop him because he was in for the fight of his life.

Abby sat quietly at the table with Max, thinking to herself and replaying the conversation she had with Adam over and over. What did he expect she would do? Drop everything and welcome him with open arms? That would not happen; it could not happen. For one thing, she had more respect for herself than that. She had to admit she still needed an explanation from Adam for why he left. She hoped that would be the closure she had needed, but wondered if there would be any possible explanation that would make her want to go back to him. She wasn't exactly sure. She knew she had feelings for Max. The more she was with him, the more she felt for him. She was just really confused with Adam telling her he had made a mistake. What's more, that he would tell her he loved her hadn't even crossed her mind.

"Penny for your thoughts," Max said to Abby softly, knowing she must be thinking about her encounter with Adam. He just wished he knew more about what they talked about before he got over there.

"I was just thinking about what a beautiful wedding it was today," Abby said, not telling him what she was really thinking.

He knew she wasn't thinking that, but didn't press her. "I agree; it was one of the nicest I've been to, but I may be a little prejudiced since this is my only one with you," Max said.

Abby smiled at Max, and said, "Me too."

Just then, one of Abby's favorite wedding songs came on; Copa Cabana. Max and Abby got back up to dance with the bride and groom. It was her duty as the maid of honor and Colleen's best friend, she figured, to party with the bride and groom until the very last guests left. Plus, she had to admit the dancing let her burn off some of the emotion she was feeling.

Colleen pulled her close and they went a little ways away from the men.

"Is everything ok, Abby?" Colleen asked her.

"Yes! Everything is great. Are you having the best day of your life?" Abby asked Colleen, trying to cleverly change the subject to avoid it. Her friend was much too smart for that.

"Forget about me, you know I am. But you, on the other hand, what's going on? What did Adam say to you?" Colleen asked her. She had a feeling Adam had said something to upset her friend.

"He told me he still loves me and wants me back," Abby told her.

"He said what!?! What does he think, that you'll drop everything and just go back to him?" She asked Abby.

"I don't know. Maybe. He's wrong though. I don't really know what to believe right now and I'm not sure what to do," Abby said.

"What do you want to do?" Colleen asked her, worried about her friend.

"I really don't know, Colleen. I do know that I don't want you to worry about it on your wedding day, though. Please don't worry about me. I'll be just fine," Abby said. Then, she changed the subject. "Are you ready for your honeymoon? Are you excited?"

"I cannot wait! I'm so happy right now." Colleen said. "But that doesn't mean I'm not here for you. If you want to talk, I'm here until tomorrow afternoon. And you can always try my cell phone while I'm gone." Colleen said, changing the subject back.

"Colleen, I will not call you on your honeymoon! Don't even tell me I can because I won't!" Abby told her.

"Oh, I know, but you know I'm here whenever you need me." Colleen reminded her.

"I know, Colleen," Abby replied, and she grabbed Colleen's hand to end the conversation and the girls made their way back to the men.

After dancing a few more slow songs with Abby, Max excused himself to go to the men's room.

Adam watched Max as he walked away, realizing it was a perfect opportunity to talk to him alone and figure out just how serious Abby was with this guy. He walked towards the men's room slowly, making sure Max entered well before Adam.

As soon as Adam walked into the men's room, he cornered Max, who was washing his hands.

"Max," Adam addressed him.

As soon as he heard his name, he knew something was up. Max turned toward Adam, and replied, "Yeah."

Adam cocked his head and looked at Max for a second before saying more, thinking about what he should say. "Have you and Abby been dating a long time?"

He wanted to know how much competition this guy would be. He was also a little pissed that his friend, Tom, the groom didn't even bother to say anything. Tom had told him when she'd been on a couple dates with some of their mutual friends, but nothing had worked out.

"A few months," Max replied, stretching it a little.

Good, that isn't long, Adam thought. "I don't know how much Abby has told you about our past." Adam said.

"Enough." Replied Max.

"You know about me, then?" Adam asked.

"I do," Max calmly told him.

"Well, I'm just giving you a warning that I'm going to do everything I can to win her back," Adam told Max.

"Is that right?" Max asked him, amazed.

"Yes," Adam replied, thinking maybe it would scare the guy off.

"Thanks for the warning." Max told him. "You must regret leaving her, Adam. You'd be dumb not to because she's amazing. But I can't help but wonder if you want her back because she's with someone else and happy?" Max asked, hoping that sent a message that he wouldn't back down easily.

Adam stared at Max, wondering just how happy she was. "No, I didn't even know she was dating anyone," Adam told him.

"Maybe that's because you haven't spoken in so long," Max shot back, and before Adam could say anything else, he continued. "If you'll excuse me, Abby is waiting." Max left Adam standing in the men's room.

As he walked towards Abby, Max plastered a smile on his face. There was no sense in telling her what happened in the bathroom.

"You okay?" Abby asked, sensing something had bothered him.

"Of course," Max replied. "You ready for more dancing?" He asked Abby, who at that time noticed Adam come out of the bathroom, a few seconds after Max.

Abby decided not to ask if anything happened in the bathroom, even though she suspected it did. She'd bring it up later. Instead, she said "Yes, let's go!"

The song "I will Survive" was playing, but ended and a slow song came on.

Max and Abby danced the rest of the night and didn't have any further run-ins with Adam, to their relief.

Abby had noticed Adam left shortly after he had come out of the bathroom after Max. When the night was finally over, Max and Abby made their way to the hotel room. The reception was in the hotel, so it didn't take long to get to their destination.

Abby was having a very hard time with the conversation she had with Adam earlier. She wondered how sincere he really was and what she should do about it. Now that she finally had someone she was truly interested in and in love with, why had he chosen to tell her all of this? She knew their conversation was far from over. But she didn't really know how everything would pan out.

Abby and Max crawled into bed and snuggled together. They talked for a long time, mostly about the wedding. They didn't talk about Adam, but Max knew she was probably thinking about him.

They both were very tired, and knowing she had a lot on her mind, Max was just going to hold Abby until they drifted off to sleep. However, as they snuggled, she started to kiss him and that changed very quickly.

Chapter 11

The Truth Will Set You Free

$\mathcal{A}$s Abby and Max drove home after seeing Colleen and Tom off to the airport, Abby decided it was a good time to ask what happened in the bathroom between Max and Adam.

"What did you and Adam talk about in the bathroom last night?" Abby asked him without any warning, startling Max.

"What do you mean?" Max asked, trying to act dumb.

"Oh, come on. You had a strange look on your face after you left the bathroom and then I saw Adam walk out right after you. What did he say to you?" Abby asked, prodding.

"Nothing, really. Just asked me if we were dating long and if I knew anything about him," Max told her.

"Hmm," Abby replied, not really believing him. "And what did you say?"

"Well, I told him I knew who he was and that we'd been dating long enough," Max told her.

She found it strange that Adam would confront Max and wondered what he was trying to accomplish. She also wondered what Max was hiding from her, as if he was trying to protect her in some way.

"So, care to share what you and Adam said at the bar last night?" Max asked, thinking since he told her about his conversation with Adam, maybe she'd open up and tell him.

"He told me he made a huge mistake and has regretted it ever since. That he still loves me. Think it's true?" Abby asked him.

"Abby, of course he regrets it," Max replied.

Abby filled him in on the rest of the conversation, not wanting to hide anything from Max. When she was done, she asked Max, "Well, what do you think?"

"I think he regrets it after seeing you again, happy and getting on with your life. I think he looks at you and realizes what he lost and wants it back. But it's not up to him, Abby, it's up to you to decide what you want to do about it." He told her.

By then, they had reached Max's parent's house. He pulled up into the driveway and put the car into park.

"I had a great time last night, Abby," Max said. "Give me a call later, okay?" Max told her. He wondered if he'd get to see her before her trip to Napa.

"I had a wonderful time with you, Max. I'll call you later," Abby said. She leaned in and gave him a kiss goodbye.

Max hopped out of the car, grabbed his bag and then with a little wave walked up to his parents' house.

Abby moved over to the driver side of the car and sat there for a minute, watching him walk up the front steps. She was more than surprised about the turn of events. Never had she thought about the possibility of Adam telling her he still loved her and that he regretted his decision.

Abby put the car in drive and then drove to her house. When she got home, she got into her pajamas, poured a glass of wine and then just sat and thought.

Maybe Adam wouldn't even call her. Maybe he was just telling her all that because he had too much to drink. He didn't seem drunk, but still, it could be possible. Or, maybe he didn't like seeing her with someone else.

She remembered the look in his eyes and he looked like he was telling her the truth. He even had tears, which she'd never seen before from him other than when he showed up the day of their wedding, even when his dad died.

An hour later, the phone rang.

"Hello," She said, waiting to hear Adam's voice.

"Hello, Abby." Adam replied. "You alone?" Adam asked her, thinking he'd have a better chance if Max hadn't gone home with her.

"Yes," She replied.

"Can we talk?" Adam asked, smiling to himself.

"Yes," She said again.

"I mean in person. Can I come over?" Adam asked her, hoping she'd say yes. He could be more convincing in person.

Abby contemplated his question. She wanted to finish the conversation they had started at the wedding reception and a phone call wouldn't allow her to see facial expressions or to see how he really felt.

"Abby?" Adam asked, because she hadn't answered yet.

"Yes, Adam, I think in person would be best. Are you coming over now?" Abby asked.

"Yes, I can be there in fifteen." Adam said.

"Okay. See you then," Abby said, and hung up.

Adam hung up the phone, nervous as hell. Was he really prepared to tell her everything? Would she be able to forgive him? He had to give it a shot, because he was very close to losing the love of his life once and for all.

♥ ♥ ♥

Abby decided pajamas were not appropriate attire for the conversation they were about to have. She quickly changed into clothes and brushed her hair and put it into a pony tail. She applied lip gloss, but nothing else. She figured he could see her the way she was and if he loved her, he wouldn't care.

Exactly fifteen minutes later, Adam showed up at her door. Abby opened the door and let him inside.

He looked incredible. He was wearing a tight t-shirt which showed every new muscle he had sculpted onto his body in the year they had been apart, designer jeans which hung down low on his hips and his hair was bleached from the sun. Abby gulped.

He had a gift with him, and it was in a very small box. She couldn't help but wonder what it was.

He pulled her into a hug and she took a moment to just feel him. God, she remembered how it was to be in his arms like it was yesterday, and he felt so good. He smelled like Adam, felt like Adam, and it made her very sad. She finally pushed him away gently.

"Sorry, Abby. I didn't mean to…," Adam said, and trailed off.

"Don't apologize. I'm just not ready for that. We have some talking to do," She replied.

They walked into her living room and they sat down on two different couches.

"Nice wedding," Adam remarked.

"Yes, it was nice," Abby replied.

"I don't know if you've done any thinking about our conversation?" Adam asked, although he must have already known the answer.

"Of course, Adam," Abby replied. "It was a bit of a shock to hear you say all that."

"I know. I'm sorry. I've lived the last year of my life regretting that decision." Adam began reciting the words he'd rehearsed over and over in his head.

She didn't say anything, so he continued. "I know I hurt you and I don't even deserve you, but I'm here because I still love you and I want another chance. I want to make it up to you," Adam told her, pleading with her. "I know you're seeing someone. I don't know how serious it is, so I don't know if I have even a chance at this, but I have to try. I'm willing to wait as long as it takes."

"This is so unexpected, Adam. It just doesn't make sense. I don't understand why, after a year, you're telling me all this now. Are you sure about this? Or maybe because you saw me with another man you just had a hard time with it. Or maybe you need closure. I need it too, Adam. This could be our closure," She replied.

"No! That's not it. I tell you, I've loved you since we first started dating and it hasn't changed. If anything, I love you more now than ever. Here, take this. I had bought it and was going to give it to you on our wedding day," Adam told her.

137

"What is it?" Abby asked.

"Open it." Adam replied.

Abby opened the gift and there in the box was a diamond earring and necklace set which matched her engagement ring. "It's beautiful, Adam."

"Where is your engagement ring?" Adam asked.

"In my jewelry box," Abby told him.

"You didn't sell it?" He asked. He knew she wasn't the type to sell it, but still had wondered.

"I was going to give it back to you eventually," Abby told him.

"I don't want it back. I want you to keep it. I want you to keep these earrings and necklace, too, no matter what happens. You deserve these," Adam told her.

"Adam, I don't know what you want from me or expect. I loved you so much and you hurt me more than anything. I need time to think. I'm dating someone right now, and it's getting serious," Abby told him. "And you still haven't told me why."

"I know. I'm ready to tell you now, Abby, but it's really hard to tell and it will be hard for you to hear," Adam warned her.

"Understood. But after a year, Adam, I'm more than ready to hear." Abby urged him.

Adam took a deep breath, and began the story he'd dreaded telling her for over a year.

"The night before the wedding, there was never a happier man in the history of the world. I was so happy to become your husband and was ready to start our lives together. The morning of our wedding I felt the same way. I was making sure my tux was ready and getting my bags packed for our trip. But then Jennifer showed up at my apartment." Adam swallowed hard, and then continued, knowing how hard this would be for Abby to hear.

Adam could see Abby's eyes register the name as being his ex-girlfriend and they had broken up shortly before he met Abby. "Abby, she told me I was a father. She had heard I was getting married and decided I needed to know. "

"What?" Abby asked, completely shocked. Things started going through her head, like how old was the child, were they a boy or a girl, why hadn't Jennifer had told him sooner, why did she wait until the day of their wedding, and a dozen other questions. She also started to think how Adam might have felt hearing that news.

"Yes, and I was shocked at first. She told me she knew without a doubt I was her daughter's father." Adam paused, and then she could see he still felt anger in some ways as he continued. "Then I became angry. I asked her how the hell she could keep that from me and then choose the day of my wedding to tell me the biggest news of my life."

"I'd like to know that myself. What did she say?" Abby asked.

Adam could remember that day well and although he was angry as hell, the look on Jennifer's face told him that she had no idea it was his actual wedding day when she flew out and told him the news. She felt horrible that she'd waited that long. She had always known it wasn't fair to him for her to hold that information to herself and the wedding was what finally made her fess up.

"Abby, she didn't know it was our wedding day, and I believe that's true. She felt horrible when she found out. She decided I needed to know before I started my life with you. She had found out through mutual friends that I was getting married but she didn't know the date. She figured I had just gotten engaged since she was just finding out. She also said she thought you should also know before you married me," Adam told her.

"Well, wasn't that sweet of her?" Abby said, sarcastically. Then, she changed her tone since it wasn't going to help matters. "I guess I'll give her the benefit of the doubt on that one. It was very wrong of her not to have told you right away, in my opinion."

"We agree on that," Adam said.

"So, what's her name?" Abby asked him softly, trying to get used to the idea of him having a child.

"Amber." Adam said.

"How old is she?" Abby asked.

"Now she's almost three but at that time she was eighteen months." Adam told her and then paused, looking for signs things would start to register for Abby that for Amber to be eighteen months on the day of their wedding, Jennifer would have gotten pregnant six months after they started dating.

Adam continued while Abby was still silent. "Needless to say, after she told me I panicked. I didn't know what to do. I knew I couldn't start a life with you when something like this was sprung on me. Had she told me a week before, I would have been able to think clearly. But I snapped, Abby. I didn't know what the hell to do," Adam told her.

"So, what happened then?" Abby asked, thinking she needed all the information before she could really react.

"She wanted me to meet Amber. And don't get me wrong, I wanted to meet her, but I also wasn't completely sure she was my daughter because this was the first I had heard of it. I was still angry I wasn't told right away I had a child." Adam said, and then continued. "My only thought was I had to find out right away if Amber was truly my daughter. And to me, that meant we couldn't get married that day. I couldn't think straight. I didn't want to tell you; I was terrified of how you'd react. Today, I know I should have told you and let you decide if you still wanted to marry me, but I felt like I was making the right decision at the time."

"Adam, this is so shocking. I go back to that day and I knew something had happened, but I couldn't figure out what could be so awful that you couldn't tell me. You should have told me, Adam. You should have trusted me," Abby told him.

"I know that now, but I panicked. Something in my mind snapped and that was the only option I saw. I didn't even tell my mother, Abby!" Adam told her, knowing Abby would understand the impact of that information since they were very close.

"So, where did you go?" She asked.

"After I left your house, I went to California, where Jennifer and Amber are living. I was first going to meet Amber and also take a DNA test to make sure she was my daughter. Jennifer told me she was positive I was her father, so I was eager to meet her right away. The whole time on the plane, all I could see was your face when I told you I couldn't marry you. It was the hardest day of my life and I hated doing it. I thought about calling you so many times to tell you what was going on, and I tried once but I got your answering machine." Adam took a deep breath and went on.

"When we landed in California, our first stop was to meet Amber. Jennifer kept calling me her daddy and I fell in love with this little girl at first sight. After playing for a few minutes, we all went to the hospital and Amber and I took our DNA tests. When they told us it would be a week to wait for results, it didn't make me happy but I decided to stay for a while and get to know Amber. In that week, I spent day and night with Amber. Yes, Jennifer was there almost the whole time, but it was mostly me and Amber. She's an amazing little girl," Adam said.

Abby could see he clearly loved the little girl very much and was happy to see Adam had such a love for his daughter. She couldn't help but smile.

"The following week the result came back and we were all together when we read them. I lost it completely; I am not Amber's father," Adam said sadly. "Ironic, isn't it? Jennifer hadn't meant to choose the day of our wedding, but she managed to have the worst timing. In the span of a week, I lost my bride, I became a father and then the daughter I loved from the second I met her was taken away from me in an instant with a DNA test result," Adam told her.

"Oh, Adam," Abby said, shaking her head. "I don't know what to say. I'm sorry you went through that, and I'm sorry Amber had to go through all that. That was horrible of Jennifer to do that to you, me and especially Amber!" Abby said, feeling very badly for both Adam and Amber.

But something was still nagging at Abby. She still couldn't see why he felt he had to call off the wedding. She wished Adam would have trusted Abby with the information. She was sure if Adam had come to her with that information the day of their wedding, they could still have gotten married, or if nothing else, choose together to postpone it. Just the fact that he had a child wasn't a reason to have him call off the wedding unless there was something else she didn't know.

Adam had tears in his eyes thinking of the little girl. "To Jennifer's defense, she really did think I was Amber's father, so when the results came back Jennifer became hysterical."

"Have you seen Amber since then?" Abby asked him.

"No. Jennifer won't let me. She won't return my calls. After several months, she changed her number and I haven't been able to find a new one for her. Shortly after her number changed, you had asked me to stop calling. I was depressed for a while," Adam told her, and he was obviously very hurt by the entire thing.

"I'm sure you were, Adam," Abby said. But something was still nagging at Abby. "Adam, something I don't understand is if Amber was only 18 months old, why did Jennifer think she was your daughter? You and I would have been dating for almost six months by then," Abby said.

"I figured you'd catch on to that one but would have told you anyway. Abby, several months after you and I started dating I saw Jennifer at a bar. She kept buying me drinks and she told me she wanted me back. I kept telling her no and that I was in a relationship, but she wouldn't listen and kept insisting she wanted me back. I don't know why it happened, it just did. I slept with Jennifer that night. I was drunk and stupid that night and made a huge mistake," Adam told her, looking down at his feet.

"Aha, I see," Abby said, thinking that things were making a little more sense now. She finally understood why he had panicked and didn't tell her the day of their wedding. To come and tell Abby he found out he had a child with an ex-girlfriend was one thing, but to find out that he had cheated on her to make that child was a whole different story. He only made everything worse by leaving and not giving her a reason right away, but she wondered if she would have been able to forgive him on the day of their wedding.

Finally, she said, "I'm glad you told me everything, Adam. And I truly feel bad for you and Amber." She tilted her head and said, "Jennifer, not so much. She's made a lot of bad decisions and it seems everyone is suffering from them." She paused, and then asked, "Is there anything else I should know?" She looked at Adam.

"No, Abby, that's it," He replied, but feeling the need to defend Jennifer for some reason, he went on to say, "But I do think Jennifer is also hurting from this, Abby."

Abby nodded her head and said, "Yes, well, you'll have to forgive me if I am having a hard time feeling bad for her," She told him. "I need time to think everything over, Adam. That was a lot of information for me to digest."

"I understand, Abby." Adam told her and got up from the couch, sensing at least this conversation was over.

Abby got up and followed him to the door.

"Before I leave, I want to tell you something." Adam said. "The night you asked me to stop calling, I drove over here. I sat in your driveway for three hours and tried to find the courage to tell you everything. It broke my heart to have you ask me to stop calling you because I knew it was a sign you were letting me go. You were trying to get on with your life. Until then, I was calling you and to hear your voice I knew there was still a change. The night you asked me to stop calling you, I knew I had lost you." Adam said, and then added, "Please think about how you feel and try to figure out if you still love me and if you could ever forgive me. I love you and want you to be my wife. I made a mistake by sleeping with Jennifer and that mistake ruined my life."

"Adam, it's a lot for me to think about. As I already said, I'm seeing someone and we're starting to get serious," Abby said.

"I understand," Adam replied.

"I do have one question, though," Abby told him.

"Yes?" Adam asked.

"Did you see anyone over the last year? Date anyone?" Abby asked him. She looked into his eyes so she could see what he'd say and know if he was telling the truth.

"I've gone out on a few dates, but nothing has been serious," Adam said, truthfully.

"Okay," She said, nodding. "I'm going away for a while. I'll call you when I get back," Abby said to him.

"Where are you going? How long will you be gone?" Adam asked her.

"I'm going on a vacation to Napa Valley. I'll be gone for over a week," Abby replied.

"Who are you going with?" Adam asked, wondering if Max would be with her, hoping not since it would definitely lower his chances.

143

"I'm going by myself. My parents booked it for me," She told him.

Adam was relieved to hear that and thought she couldn't be too serious with Max if he wasn't going with her. "Abby, can I request one more thing?" Adam asked her, and when he got her nod, he added, "Can I please hug you again?"

She hesitated, and then nodded her head yes.

He wasted no time and pulled her into one of his familiar hugs. He smelled so good, and he put his hand on the back of her head like he always had. It brought back very happy memories of their life together. She closed her eyes and let him hug her for a minute, even hugging him back.

He finally let her go and for a second she thought he might kiss her so she stepped back and said, "Goodnight Adam."

"I won't call you, but I'll be waiting for your call," Adam replied.

"Okay," Abby told him. There wasn't much more to really say to him until she'd had time to think.

She had finally gotten the explanation she had needed for over a year and was almost sorry she had it. Everything he told her made her heart break for him and for Amber. She never thought it could be possible, but Adam's explanation actually had her thinking she could possibly forgive him for leaving her on their wedding day. It didn't help that he had cheated on her when they were dating, but she was going to try to put that one behind her for now.

Abby sat down on the couch and with tears in her eyes looked over at the diamond set Adam had given her. What the hell was she supposed to do now?

♥ ♥ ♥

Abby wished Colleen was there with her to help her get through this tough time. She'd know exactly what to do. She had started to fall in love with Max, and thought life was so unfair to have thrown her this cruel hand. She didn't know if things would work out with her and Max but wanted a chance to figure it out.

She decided she wanted to hear Max's voice and dialed his number. She had wanted to see him one more time before she left, but wasn't sure if she'd get the chance. Her parents were driving her to the airport in the morning.

Max answered on the third ring. "Hey there, stranger."

"Hi, Max," Abby replied.

"How are you?" Max asked.

"Well, Adam was just here," Abby replied, dreading how the conversation would go. She decided to get it over with.

"Oh?" Max asked.

Abby told him everything Adam had told her, including him cheating on her while they were dating.

"Well? What do you think of that?" Abby asked him.

"It's all shocking, to say the least," Max said and admittedly thinking that aside from him cheating on her, that was a pretty good reason for his behavior on their wedding day. "I don't know what to say. I guess you need to decide if you can forgive him and if so, what that would mean."

"What do you mean?" Abby asked.

"Well, if you forgive him, does that mean you'd give him another chance? Or does that mean you forgive what he did but you still can't go back to him?"

"I can forgive him, but after that I'm not quite sure," Abby said, and left the rest unsaid.

Max just nodded his understanding. "I see. I think your trip couldn't have come at a better time," Max told her.

Abby agreed whole-heartedly. "Thank you, Max, for understanding. I think you're right about the trip," Abby said.

"I just have one more thing to say, something you need to take into consideration. We may have only been dating a couple months, but in that time, I have fallen in love with you. You're kind, generous, a fantastic cook, you're amazing with my parents and you are the prettiest woman I've ever laid eyes on," Max told her. "I don't think Adam deserves a second chance, but I guess I'm a little biased. That's up to you to decide and make the decision that's right for you. I'll be here when you get back from your trip."

145

"Thank you. I have a lot to think about on my trip. Goodbye Max," Abby said.

"Goodbye, Abby," Max said, and gently hung up the phone.

Abby looked at the phone in her hand as the tears welled up in her eyes. Max knew she had a decision to make and she knew he was trying to be understanding. It was the hardest, most important decision of her life and she knew that. She agreed with Max the trip was coming at a good time because she needed this time on her own to think everything through.

Chapter 12

A Much Needed Break

That night after packing for her trip to Napa Valley, Abby thought about her past relationship with Adam. Some of the memories were really great ones, like one of their first dates at the zoo. It made her laugh just thinking about it, because it was apparently mating season at the zoo and in almost every exhibit they visited they were treated to a different view of the mating rituals. Lions and gorillas and even the zebras took their turns mating in front of them. It was such a funny day and they laughed almost the entire date.

She went to the closet in her spare bedroom and took out the box she'd packed away containing some of Adam's belongings. She had packed up the box the night she asked Adam to stop calling her. Now, a year later, she finally felt it was time to go through the box and that she'd be able to do it without breaking down.

Smiling, she looked inside the box and started carefully taking everything out. With each item came a different memory of her past with Adam.

The first piece was Adam's sweatshirt, which made her think of when they had watched a movie at the old drive-in and it had gotten very chilly so he had given it to her to wear. She had never given it back to Adam before he left and she was glad for that. After he left, she would put on his sweatshirt and because it still smelled like him it had made her feel close to him. She lifted the sweatshirt up to her nose and inhaled. She could no longer detect Adam's scent.

Abby set aside the sweatshirt and took out the next thing. It was a copy of the CD of Adam's favorite band; Pearl Jam. She put the CD on top of the sweatshirt. The next one was a Steven King novel Adam had been reading when he'd sleep over at her house. He never finished it.

The next thing brought tears to her eyes. She reached in the box and took out the turtle statue Abby bought for herself the day Adam had proposed. Holding the turtle brought her back to one of the happiest memories she had of Adam.

Abby closed her eyes as she thought about that day. Adam had taken her to the Como zoo in St. Paul and led her to the beautiful gardens in the conservatory. It was one of their favorite places to go.

Two Years earlier

As they walked through the conservatory, Abby told Adam, "I love it here."

"I know," Adam replied. "It's one of my favorite places to go with you".

"The flowers, they're just so beautiful," She said.

"You are beautiful, Abby," Adam replied, taking her hand as they kept walking.

Abby just blushed, but didn't say anything.

They kept walking to the back of the conservatory and they noticed all of the turtles sunning themselves on the rocks. Adam stopped all of a sudden by Abby's favorite water lilies and got down on one knee. He put his hand in his pocket and pulled out a small box.

Abby looked down at him, realizing what he was doing.

"Abby, I love you very much. I want to spend the rest of my life with you. Will you marry me?" Adam asked her as he opened the box to show her a beautiful round cut diamond solitaire on a band of platinum. A few weeks before, Adam had taken one of the rings she usually wore on her right hand ring finger and had tried it on to get a feel for her size.

He was able to slip it partly on his pinkie finger and that's how he had them size the ring, hoping it would be the right fit.

Abby's face lit up as she answered him. "I love you too, Adam. Yes!" Adam slipped the ring on her finger and it fit her perfectly.

As they were leaving that day, Abby and Adam had stopped in the gift shop and found the little statues of zoo animals for sale. Abby couldn't pass up buying one of the turtles to always remind her of the day Adam proposed.

♥ ♥ ♥

Abby opened her eyes and looked down at the turtle in her hand, thinking she'd never again be able to see a turtle without remembering that day.

She finally went through the rest of the box, which was filled with different items she was sure he wouldn't even want back; a toothbrush and toothpaste, an old razor with shaving cream, cologne, and a few other personal items. They were more or less just everyday items which she remembered him using very clearly.

Abby put everything back in the box and added her beautiful engagement ring and the necklace and earring set he'd given her that morning. She wasn't sure what to do with all of it quite yet.

Abby finally decided she'd better try to get to sleep, so she put her suitcases and carry-on luggage by the door, ready for the morning flight, and then headed off to bed. She thought about asking Max to bring her but she decided she wanted her parents to send her off, especially since they had planned the whole thing and paid for it.

As she drifted off to sleep that night, she couldn't help but think about Adam and wonder if she'd be able to forgive him.

♥ ♥ ♥

Max thought about going to the airport in the morning to see Abby off to Napa, but decided against it. He figured Abby needed time on her own and her trip was the perfect opportunity. He'd miss her very much but there wasn't much else he could do but wait.

Max tried to stay busy while Abby was gone. His mom and dad were getting better settled and he had started looking more seriously at lots and homes for sale in the area.

He also took the opportunity to call a couple of his buddies from high school. They met up one night at the "Time Out" bar in Elk River.

They talked for hours about old times and what they were all doing now. He told them about Abby and they all remembered her. They laughed that she had finally gotten what she'd always wanted; him. He learned more about some of the things they did to Abby as they were growing up, especially what Pete would do. Most of the other guys gave up after Max left for college because it wasn't fun to tease her anymore. He got a renewed sense of anger at Pete.

As the night wrapped up and he was just about to leave, he noticed Adam having a drink at the bar with another woman. He found it interesting that he'd be there with another woman when he had just told Abby he hadn't dated anyone in the year since they had broken up.

Max decided to just leave without saying anything but as he was walking out, Adam noticed Max.

In a split second decision, Adam decided to try and put the odds in his favor a little, thinking if Max was out of the way, maybe he'd have a better chance of her forgiving him. He figured Abby still had five days left of her trip and decided to make Max think he was meeting her there for a nice long romantic weekend.

"Max, how are you? This is a friend of mine, Sarah. Hey, Sarah's single. Maybe you two should hook up, huh?" Adam said to Max. Max looked over at Sarah and she smiled at him with interest.

"I'm fine, thanks. Hi Sarah, nice to meet you. Sorry, Sarah, Adam's just kidding around. He knows I have a girlfriend," Max told her, and then looked back at Adam.

"A girlfriend?" Adam asked him, and then before Max could say anything, he continued. "I hope you're not talking about Abby. I wouldn't consider her your girlfriend, Max." Adam said, chuckling as if Max were being ridiculous.

"Oh yeah? Why's that, Adam?" Max asked, wanting to refuse taking his bait, but also wanting to hear what he had to say.

Sarah looked back and forth at the two men and decided to high-tail it out of there. "I gotta go, Adam. See ya."

They both ignored her as she walked away.

"Um, because I just booked a flight to Napa Valley to meet Abby for a long weekend. I'm pretty sure she wouldn't want me to join her if she still thought you were an item." Adam told him, treating him like he was an idiot. Then, turning the knife a little more, said "Plus, she told me she was going to call you and tell you she had made her decision. She hasn't called you yet?"

Max just looked at Adam, wondering if any of it was true. "Is that right?" He asked.

"I'm actually leaving tomorrow." Adam said.

Max just looked at him and then said, "Tell Abby I said hi." Then he walked out of the bar.

As Adam watched Max leave, he thought perhaps he shouldn't have told Max that lie, but then quickly decided he was glad. As the saying goes, all is fair in love and war. He was doing it for the woman he loved and using it as a way to get back what they had before he made the biggest mistake of his life. Jennifer had ruined his chances with Abby a year ago, so he thought it was only fair to make his chances with her now a little better.

♥ ♥ ♥

Abby's trip was exactly what she needed and exactly what she had dreamed of. She toured the Robert Mondavi winery, took a bus charter tour of a couple smaller vineyards, ate at a different place for every meal and tried every dessert she could possibly find. She was sure she would have gained 10 pounds from her trip if she hadn't walked so much.

Her favorite part of the trip was the ride on the hot air balloon overlooking several vineyards. Along with the man flying the balloon there was a married couple celebrating their 25th wedding anniversary.

After all of the introductions, Abby asked the couple, "So how long have you been married?"

"Twenty five years, although it feels like five!" Robert said, looking lovingly at his wife, Anna.

"Or maybe ten?" Anna teased him.

"Do you have children?" She asked them.

"Three wonderful kids, all grown and out of the house now, though. Jack is 23, Julie is 21 and Jacob is 19." Anna told her.

"Do you have someone, Abby?" Robert asked her.

"Huh, that's quite the story. I won't bore you with it," Abby said.

Just then, the air balloon ride operator told them they were gliding over another vineyard and told them to look at all of the workers in the field.

When he was silent again and they were all looking over the fields, Anna said, "So, tell us the story, Abby."

"Are you sure? It complicated," Abby told them.

"Tell us." Robert said.

So Abby gave them a skimmed down version of her life as she saw it, including the latest details she learned from Adam and how she thought she was falling in love with Max.

Robert and Anna looked at each other and nodded in agreement.

"So? What do you think?" Abby asked them.

"Well, it's not our place to say anything about it or sway your mind in any way because that's your decision. You need to make the right decision for you, not anyone else. Follow your heart, Abby." Anna said.

"So how have you been able to stay together so long?" Abby asked her.

Anna and Robert looked at each other and smiled. "Well, first off we love each other and there hasn't been a day that's gone by without telling each other just that. We're best friends and we tell each other pretty much everything. Don't get me wrong; it hasn't all been roses over the years but we've always gotten through everything that was thrown our way because we did it together. And above all else, we've always trusted each other. Trust is one of the most important things in a marriage; without trust, the rest wouldn't have been possible."

Abby just nodded, understanding what she was saying and not surprisingly was in complete agreement.

Many of the nights in Napa were so comfortable that she lit a fire outside and sat there reading her favorite novel, "Can You Keep a Secret" by Sophie Kinsella, while sipping wine from the wineries she'd visited during the day. Those were nights where Abby felt like she needed to escape from her problems.

She missed Max very much and thought about him a lot.

She loved that they had fun no matter what they did. They had so much in common that pretty much everything he suggested turned out to be a blast. She smiled as she thought about one of her favorite dates with Max when they went to the drag races in Brainerd and Max let her drive his Camaro in the Powder Puff races. It was easy to let her mind think back to that date, which was very shortly before Colleen's wedding.

A couple weeks earlier...

Max was just about to hop in his car and race again when he looked over at Abby and asked, "Do you want to ride with me?"

"Really? Yes, I'd love to go. Won't it slow you down?" She asked.

"Not really. Come on, let's go!" Max said, excited she wanted to drive with him.

"Yay!" Abby said, clapping her hands in excitement and then put on his spare helmet and hopped in the car with him.

Max staged the car, getting it in between the two posts to put it into position. He got a yellow light indicating he was correctly staged. As they were waiting for the other car, she watched how Max's feet were on both the clutch and gas and he had it in first gear. He turned to Abby and said, "You want to get it revved up and ready for when that green light hits. The lights go fast so watch them."

Abby looked up at the lights and watched as they changed from yellow to green. The red one on the bottom was if you took off too early before the green hit. Max let up on the clutch to get started as soon as he possibly could. And then they were off, screaming down the track.

Max expertly changed gears until his car was travelling at a very fast speed. He managed to beat the Pontiac GTO to the finish line in 12.06 seconds. After Max got the car stopped, he turned to look at Abby to see if she enjoyed the ride and to his delight she had a huge smile on her face.

"That was awesome!" Abby said excitedly. "Can we do it again?"

"Of course. Actually, do you know how to drive a stick?" Max asked, getting an idea.

"Yes. Why?" She asked.

"Well, they have a Powder Puff race starting in a couple hours. Would you want to try driving in it?" Max asked her.

"You'd trust me with your car?" She asked him.

"Why not? If you want to try, you should ride with me again and get the hang of it. Then, we explore Brainerd and get lunch and you can drive to get the feel for my car," Max told her.

"Well, let's do that and you can decide if I drive your car well enough to enter into the race, okay?" Abby said, unsure of herself, figuring the other women in the race would have done it multiple times and she didn't want to look stupid.

Abby rode with Adam on two more races and then she drove them to Green Mill for lunch. Afterward, Abby hopped back into the driver's seat, giving Max a little smile.

"I like your car, Max." She told him.

"Then you'll love driving the quarter mile," Max said and saw the skeptical look on her face. "You can do this Abby! You did great driving this. I bet you'll kick butt on that track!" Max encouraged her.

Abby looked at Max and knew he was completely serious. He really believed in her. "Okay, what the hell? I think I can at least make it to the finish line. I'll do it," Abby said.

When they got back to the track, she signed up for the Powder Puff race, which would start in the next hour. She was nervous but very excited.

"Can you ride with me?" Abby asked Max.

"If you want me to, of course I will," Max told her.

"Yes, I want you to ride with me," Abby said.

"How about if I ride with the first time and then if you win and go to the next round, you go on your own?" Max asked her. He really thought she'd do really well racing his car, and it made him feel very proud.

"Let's just get through this first race before we have me winning the trophy, huh?" Abby said, teasing Max.

"You're going to win first place." He told her.

When it was finally time for the Powder Puff race, like an expert she drove up to the track and got into line with all of the other women. There were Buicks, Pontiacs, Chevys and multiple other hot rod models. It was fun to watch all of the women getting their cars ready to race.

As each race started, the cars in line all moved up until Abby was finally told to stage Max's Camaro. Max was surprised at how well Abby got his car staged and got the yellow light to indicate the car was in the right position.

"Okay, the other car just staged. You ready?" He asked Abby, nervous for her.

"I guess so!" Abby said, watching the lights. She pushed down on the clutch and the gas and then as soon as she saw that second yellow light, she let off the clutch and the car flew forward just as the light turned green.

Max couldn't believe Abby and how she shifted the gears of his car, as if she'd been driving it all her life. She managed to get down the track, winning the race by a couple seconds with a time of 13.26.

Abby looked at Max after she got the car stopped and asked, "Did I win?"

"Did you win? Abby, you knocked her socks off!" Max told her, excitedly.

"So I'll go on to the next round then?" Abby asked.

Max didn't say anything but nodded his head yes in amazement.

As they pulled back around the track and got back in line for the next round, the other ladies in line started clapping for her and said she had a .6 reaction time, which was almost perfect.

Abby raced several more times, and although she didn't win first place, she got second place. More than anything, she was glad she tried because she had a blast doing it. Max was so excited at her success that he promised they'd go back again before the summer was over.

♥ ♥ ♥

Abby's mind switched back to the present as the fire in the backyard of her little cottage let off a loud crackle. She couldn't help but smile at the memory and almost reached for the phone to call Max.

Instead of calling Max, Abby's mind switched to Adam and everything he had told her before her trip. Before she learned the reason he left her on the day of their wedding, Abby was sure there wasn't anything he'd be able to tell her that could make her ever think she could forgive him. But hearing everything, she realized she wasn't the only one hurt in the whole ordeal.

Yes, he handled it poorly, but he had a bomb dropped on him on the day of his wedding. She could see how much he was hurting by what Jennifer had done. Finding out he had cheated on her with Jennifer six months after they started dating was disturbing to her and she knew it was why he couldn't tell her on their wedding day.

She thought back to the night of their groom's dinner and how happy they had been together that night. She smiled at the memory, thinking of the toast he gave. It made her feel so special, so loved.

One year earlier...

"Abby and I would like to thank everyone for coming tonight. We know our closest friends and family are here and we're happy to share this night with you." Adam said, repeating the words they agreed he'd say. They all rose their glasses and cheered.

But then he surprised Abby by continuing and looking right in her eyes. "Abby, you may only be one person in the world, but you are the person to make my world complete. I love you with all my heart and

I will do everything in my power to make you smile every day for the rest of your life."

Abby had gotten tears in her eyes, and just said, "I love you too."

The memory of their grooms' dinner somehow reminded her of the time she and Adam had gone snow tubing at Bunker Hills. It was the first time he ever told her he loved her.

Two and a half years earlier...

"Are you ready, Abby?" Adam asked her, holding their tubes at the top of the snow-covered hill.

Abby looked down the hill at the hills and jumps made in the snow. "As long as we don't go over a jump our first time down the hill, okay?" Abby asked him.

"Of course not, although I know you'll love that part too," Adam told her, smiling.

Adam looked at Abby, thinking she looked very pretty in her rose-colored Columbia Sportswear jacket, matching hat and mittens, black snow pants, and black boots. It was a beautiful winter day. Adam figured it was a little over 30 degrees, which was very warm for January in Minnesota.

They got their tubes ready at the top of the hill, hopped on and then held on to the strings of each other's tubes so they could go down together.

Abby laughed the entire way down the hill, thinking Adam was probably right that she'd also love the jumps! When they finally got down the hill and the tubes came to a stop, Adam jumped up off his tube and then held out his hand to help Abby up. As he pulled her up, he took her into his arms and gave her a kiss.

"Did you like it?" Adam asked her.

"Yes! Let's do it again!" She told him. "But this time let's go over the jumps."

Adam laughed at that, and said, "I love you."

Abby looked up into Adam's eyes, and knew he meant it. She had known she loved him for a while, but hadn't wanted to say anything for fear of scaring him away. "I love you too."

As they looked at each other, neither of them realized they were still standing in the way of other tubers. All of a sudden, they were knocked off their feet by a teenager who had gone down the hill. They laughed hysterically when the poor kid apologized to them.

The memory made Abby smile again.

♥ ♥ ♥

By the time she spent her last day in Napa Valley, Abby had forgiven Adam, but knew she never really had a decision to make between the men in her life.

Abby couldn't stop thinking about trust and about what the couple on the hot air balloon ride had told her. If there's no trust, none of it would be possible.

She was glad she finally knew what happened with Adam, but trust was the issue, on both sides. He hadn't had enough confidence in her to handle the news on their wedding day and she didn't know if she'd ever be able to faith in Adam again. Even without Max in the picture, she couldn't trust Adam. She wasn't choosing between two men but she was choosing not to be with Adam.

Chapter 13

Home Sweet Home

*A*bby got home from her trip in the afternoon and wanted very much to see Max. She quickly showered and got ready, excited to see him. She decided she'd surprise him instead of calling, hoping he'd be around.

Abby drove over to Max's parent's house, getting more excited the closer she got. She pulled up to Max's parent's house and got out of the car. She walked up the sidewalk, jumped up the steps with energy she couldn't suppress and rang the doorbell. Max came to the door and looked at her, surprised to see her.

"Oh. Abby. Hi. What are you doing here?" Max asked her. Abby sensed he was upset with her and figured it was because she hadn't called for her entire trip. She vowed to make it up to him.

"Actually, I was hoping I could steal you away for a little while. Did I come at a bad time?" Abby asked him.

"Actually, I'm just on my way out the door. Can I give you a call later?" He asked her, thinking she looked amazing with the California tan. She looked so relaxed and happy.

"Oh," She paused, disappointed and sensing something was wrong, "Is everything okay?" She asked Max.

"Yup," He replied, nodding. "Just can't talk now. Okay?"

"Okay, well, I guess give me a call when you get a chance?" Abby asked him, sad that he didn't seem happy at all to see her. She wanted to see him so badly and missed him very much. She didn't call him her whole trip and maybe that was a mistake. But she thought he understood and that he wasn't expecting her to call.

Max watched Abby walk away. He didn't want to hear about her trip because then he'd have to hear about her choosing Adam over him. It hurt to think about it.

Abby walked away from Max, wondering when he might call her. It was like he had no desire to see her. What the hell had happened while she was gone?

As she drove home, she decided to call Adam and ask if he could come over. She needed to end it, once and for all. It wasn't fair to leave him hanging, either. Regardless of the frosty reception she had received from Max, she had already made her decision. It really had nothing to do with Max, although she'd honestly be very upset if things didn't work out for them.

As soon as Abby got home, she called Adam.

"Hi Adam," Abby told him.

"You're back! I missed you," He told her. While she was gone, he started to regret telling Max he was going to be going out to Napa. It was a lie and he shouldn't have done it. How could he expect Abby to trust him again by pulling that? He hoped it wouldn't ruin his chances.

"I was hoping you could come over?" Abby asked him.

"Yes, I can come over." Adam told her. "Do you want me to come now?"

"If that works for you," Abby said.

"Be right there." Adam replied.

Abby went into her room and grabbed the box full of Adam's stuff, including her engagement ring and diamond earring and necklace set he had recently given her. She was glad to finally be closing that chapter of her life, but it also made her sad. She wasn't sure how he was going to react to her decision, but she was sure she was making the right one.

Adam arrived very quickly, faster than she had wanted because she was still mentally preparing herself for the conversation they were about to have.

Abby opened the door and Adam walked in, giving her a hug and surprising her with a kiss. Abby lightly pushed him back.

They walked into the living room and sat down on the couch.

"Well, how was your trip?" Adam asked her.

"It was great!" Abby quickly explained a few things about her trip, skimming over highlights of her hot air balloon ride and the cute cottage she stayed in.

"So, have you made any decisions, Abby?" Adam asked her, eager to hear what she had decided.

"Yes, I have," She said, and then continued. "Adam, I'm so glad that you finally told me everything. I wish on our wedding day you would have trusted me enough to come to me with everything."

"I wish I had too and I regret that very much." Adam told her.

"I forgive you, Adam." Abby started. She saw Adam's face light up, but then she continued, "But I don't think I can trust you."

"With time, I will earn your trust back, Abby," Adam told her, hopeful.

"I don't think so, Adam," Abby said, shaking her head. She truly did feel bad because he had been hurt in all of this too. It made her sad to think she was now the one hurting him.

Adam shook his head and got up from the couch. "You need more time to think. We need to go out a few times and in time you will trust me again. I won't let you tell me no until you've given me a chance to prove myself to you."

"Adam, I already made my decision. I don't need more time," Abby told him.

"How can you make a decision already? You haven't given me another chance!" Adam said, feeling desperate.

"I haven't given you a second chance? You had over a year and multiple chances, Adam, so don't put this on me!" Abby replied angrily.

"Abby, I'm leaving now. Think more about it before making up your mind. I love you and won't give up that easily," Adam said, and then left without taking no for an answer.

Abby just shook her head, thinking she'd just have to try explaining again the next time she talked to him.

♥ ♥ ♥

Max regretted sending Abby away the whole day. He felt bad because she genuinely looked hurt. But she had hurt him by lying to him or at least omitting the truth. He'd been stewing over what Adam had told him for the past six days and he was not a happy guy. Even his dad had told him to get out of the house and not come back until his mood had improved, which was unlike his dad so he figured he must have been horrible to be around.

He ended up taking a walk, and thinking about Abby. Part of his anger was that she hadn't told him about Adam meeting her in Napa yet, although admittedly he hadn't given her a chance. Mostly he was hurt because he really thought they had something special.

They had been dating for a few months but he already knew he loved her. And then Adam walked back into her life, finally giving her the explanation she needed.

He had to admit it would have been very intimidating to find out you have a kid and find out she was the age that would be a telltale sign he'd cheated. But he thought Adam should have been able to come clean with Abby that day instead of leaving her at the altar.

Max didn't sleep that night, because he couldn't get Abby's hurt look out of his mind. He watched the clock on his bedside table, passing away the time.

Finally at 6:00am, he called Abby, and she obviously had been sleeping.

"Care for a hike?" He asked her. He would rather get it over with, if she was going to break it off with him.

"Hmm, what time is it?" Abby asked, sleepily, knowing this was her last day in a while to sleep in.

"Six. I couldn't sleep," Max said.

"Oh. Are you going to come over right now?" She asked, still sleepy but awake enough to be glad he had called her.

"Is that ok? You alone?" He asked, wondering if Adam was there with her.

"Alone?" She asked, confused. "Yeah," She replied sleepily, too tired to really think more about it. "See you in a little bit."

She got up and took a quick shower, which woke her up a little more, and she started thinking about his phone call. She couldn't help but think something was strange. She pulled her hair back into a pony tail and put on her hiking gear.

Shortly after she was dressed and drinking a cup of coffee, Max rang the doorbell.

"Hey there, stranger!" Abby said, lunging at him with a hug. Max gave her a little pat and then backed away. Abby looked at Max and had enough of the cold shoulder treatment, especially because she didn't even know what she had done wrong.

She narrowed her eyes and looked at him. "Okay, what gives? Why are you mad at me? Is it because I didn't call you on my trip? I didn't think you'd be mad at me for that. You told me to call you when I got back," Abby said. She wasn't going to go hiking when he was sulking.

"Nah, why would I be mad? Ready to go?" Max told her sarcastically, and then turned and walked out her door.

She walked to the car behind him. She had no idea what was going on, but she wanted to know now. She could tell he was mad at her but had no clue why.

"Max, what the hell is going on?" Abby asked him, completely confused by his anger, and even more so why he wouldn't say why he was mad in the first place.

"Nothing," Max replied. "Get in."

"No, Max, I will not get in the car until you tell me what's wrong," Abby said firmly.

"There's nothing wrong, Abby," Max replied, unconvincingly. "So, how is Adam?" Max asked, trying to turn the conversation towards him to give her an opening.

"Fine, I guess," Abby replied.

"So you saw him then?" Max asked her.

"Yes, but it didn't go exactly as I was expecting," Abby told him, but didn't feel like talking about Adam. She wanted to know what was going on in Max's head.

Max didn't say anything, but snuck a peek at her, wondering how she'd tell him about Adam joining her on her trip. As he looked at her, he couldn't help but think about how pretty she looked that morning.

They sat in silence for a few moments. "Thank you." Abby finally said, deciding to try another angle.

"For what?" He asked her harshly, confused.

"For respecting me enough to let me go on my trip and be on my own for a while. I'm really sorry if you wanted me to call while I was gone. I thought you told me to take my time and enjoy my trip." She told him, still completely confused by his behavior.

"I knew you needed some time alone," Max told her, pausing. Then, realizing he was being a jerk, he asked her softly, "So, how was it?"

Abby noticed his tone change a little and thought maybe telling him thank you had gotten him over being mad at her.

"It was amazing!" Abby started talking and didn't stop for five minutes, thinking she'd cheer him up. She told him all about her tours and hot air balloon ride, the people she met and the desserts. "I can't wait to make some of the desserts. I know I can figure out the recipes. I wish you could have been there!" She told him.

"Oh? Wouldn't three have been a crowd?" He asked sarcastically. Not once did she mention Adam being there. He supposed she wouldn't say much about that, though.

"Huh? What do you mean?" She asked, now completely confused. Max didn't answer her.

"So, what else did you do on your trip?" Max asked her, dying to know, even though he didn't want to know too many details. His patience only ran so far.

"I did a lot of thinking, Max, that's for sure." She told him.

"And?" Max asked, trying to lead her to tell him about Adam joining her.

"Admittedly, this has been hard on me. I had no idea why Adam left that day and finally finding out was a shock. And I now understand why Adam felt like he couldn't marry me that day. It doesn't excuse the fact that he cheated, but I do understand his point of view." Abby began.

He wanted Abby to get to the point, to finally tell him about Adam meeting her in Napa. "And you must have forgiven him in order to invite him to Napa, huh?" Max asked, finally asking her point blank.

Abby paused for a minute, looked over at Max and wondered if she heard him right. Abby asked. "What did you say?"

"I ran into Adam right before he was heading to Napa Valley to meet you. He told me you had called him and asked him to spend the weekend with you there. So you don't have to hide it any longer," Max said.

Abby was at first surprised, but when she put the pieces together, it dawned on her. Replaying their conversation in her mind, she figured out why Max was so upset. It was also why he asked her if she was alone when he called that morning.

"Oh my God, Max." She felt bad that Max thought that all along, and grabbed for his hand as she told him "He lied, Max."

"Oh, come on! Tell me the truth!" Max said, mad she was still not coming clean with him.

"Adam was not in Napa with me. He lied!" Abby repeated.

"You said you saw him, Abby, but that you didn't get want you had hoped from him. Make up your mind," Max said, although in his gut started to think she was telling him the truth.

"Yes, Max, I saw Adam, but I didn't see him in Napa. I saw him yesterday." Abby's eyes narrowed as she realized that he still didn't know if he should believe her and it made her angry.

"Huh?" Max asked her, confused.

"Max, let me clear it up for you, but it's the last time I'll say it. He lied to you. He was not in Napa with me. I was alone. You can either believe me or we can end this conversation right now, but I refuse to be called a liar when I haven't lied!" Abby told him angrily.

Max looked at Abby and the realization hit; she was telling him the truth. He put his head in his hands and counted to 10 because he was so angry he wanted to punch something.

"Abby, I'm so sorry," Max told her. "Since seeing Adam, I've been waiting to hear from you and waiting for you to tell me you decided to get back together with him. He even told me where you were staying. I've been stewing for days until I was so mad I couldn't stand it! I'm sorry I didn't believe you right away," Max told her, grabbing her hands.

"I had told him I was going on a trip to Napa Valley before I left," Abby told him. She understood why Max was so upset and she couldn't blame him. It also confirmed the decision she had made about Adam. To have Adam lie to Max about meeting her in Napa affirmed her conclusion that she could not trust Adam.

"What a fool," Max said.

"No, Adam was wrong and was a total jerk for telling you that. He was very convincing, obviously. Had I known what he told you, I would have cleared it up yesterday." She told him, looking into his eyes.

"No, I meant me. I'm a fool," Max told her, looking embarrassed but relieved.

"Yes, well, I won't argue with that," Abby said, grinning at him, happy she finally figured out why he had been so upset.

"I'm sorry, Abby. I should have asked you about it right away," Max told her.

"Yes, well, we would have avoided this whole fight," Abby replied.

"It wasn't a fight; just a misunderstanding," Max told her.

"I disagree. It was our first real fight. But hey, at least it was over soon," Abby argued.

"Fine, you win, it was our first fight," Max said, and then he looked at Abby, leaned in to give her the first kiss they had in almost two weeks.

Abby pulled away from Max, raised her eyebrows and said, "But this also means we get to make up." Since they were still in her driveway, they decided to skip the hike and go inside and make up some more.

♥ ♥ ♥

Abby enjoyed spending every spare minute she had with Max. He was starting to look for a place of his own and they went to many open houses and showings, trying to find what would make the perfect house for Max. It was very fun to be part of the hunt, and she was learning a lot about what he valued in a property.

Abby soon realized that what Max wanted most of all was a home on a large piece of land. He wanted at least three bedrooms, preferably four, a three-car garage, a huge master bedroom and a modern kitchen with all the best appliances.

"I found a lot I want to show you, one that's not too far away but far enough that it's a larger lot. It's a 10 acre property in Zimmerman. How about that?" Max asked her,

"Good! Can we go look at it now?" Abby asked him.

"Let's go," Max replied.

They drove the short distance to Zimmerman, driving past many farms, including Elk and Ostrich farms. They finally found their way to the wooded lot he had found, only five miles away from the town. It was a lake-lot and was absolutely beautiful. She didn't think he could find anything nicer than what'd she was seeing.

"So what do you think?" Max asked her, after giving her a minute to look over the land.

"I think it's breath-taking. You should get this lot. It's totally perfect for you!" Abby told Max, her eyes glowing.

"Too late," Max told her.

"It's already sold?" Abby asked, disappointed, wondering why he'd even show her a sold lot.

"Yup. Sold," Max said, trying to fake disappointment.

"Oh, too bad," Abby said.

"Not really. I bought it," Max told her.

Abby's face lit up and she gave him a huge smile. "Really? It's yours?"

"Yes," Max told her, grinning, although he was thinking theirs, not just his.

"That's so great! Congratulations! When will you start building?" She asked him.

"I have to finish the plans and find a builder, but that's getting close. I think in the next month we'll be breaking ground." He told her.

"I'm so excited for you!" She told him.

Max just looked at Abby, thinking he was excited for both of them. He was really hoping she'd like it because he eventually saw them living there, raising children and growing old together. He didn't want to scare her with those thoughts so he kept them to himself. Now that she was done with Adam, they'd be able to get more serious.

After they walked around the lot together, they decided to head back to town. Max dropped Abby off at her house, giving her a soft kiss goodbye.

♥ ♥ ♥

Abby opened her door and walked inside her house, getting the sense that Max was showing her the land to get her approval. She wondered how Max saw their future. Did he see her at his new home? It made her want to end things with Adam, once and for all. She had thought a lot about Adam over the last couple days, and she hadn't changed her mind.

Abby stared at the phone and when she was just about ready to give Adam a call, her phone rang. It startled her, making her jump.

Abby answered the phone and was even more surprised to hear Adam on the other end.

"Abby, it's Adam."

"Oh. Hi," Abby replied. "I was just about to call you."

"Oh, good. Can I come over?"

"Yes." Abby answered.

"Be right there." Adam said, and hung up.

Adam got in his car and started it up, thinking this time he had to come prepared. He stopped at the florist in town and bought a dozen red roses.

♥ ♥ ♥

Abby finally heard the doorbell ring, and got up to answer the door, pausing before she opened it to collect herself. She put on a large smile and opened the door.

"Hi Adam."

"Hi. These are for you." Adam said, handing her the roses.

"Thank you, Adam," Abby told him. He had often given her roses while they were dating and engaged. It made her sad to think he was giving them to her now for the last time at the end of their relationship.

"How are you?" Adam asked her.

Abby just nodded and said, "Good." She paused and then said, "Adam, I've done a lot of thinking since our conversation the other day." Abby began.

"Yes, me too." Adam replied, nodding. "I've been thinking everything. Life with you was great and life without you was horrible. The last year has been really hard for me."

"Yes, I'm sure it has been, almost as hard as it has been on me," Abby said, reminding him he wasn't the only one hurt.

"I know it's my fault and I'm so very sorry for that. I never stopped loving you and I just hope you'll give me another chance." Adam said, pleading.

"Adam, I do still love you, but in a different way now. It's a chapter in my life that has ended. I can't be with you for many reasons." Abby began, and Adam interrupted.

"It's that Max guy, isn't it?" He asked, not listening.

"No, actually, my decision wasn't about Max at all," Abby said, and then continued, "But to be honest, having you tell him that you were meeting me in Napa didn't exactly help your cause," Abby said to him, watching his face.

Adam had the decency to look ashamed. "Yes, I know. I shouldn't have told him that and I regretted it after I did. But I wanted you to give me another chance and didn't want him in the way. I know it was wrong and I'm sorry."

"But that's just another reason I can't trust you, Adam. Don't you see that?" Abby asked him, wondering if he could grasp that trust was the whole reason she couldn't give him the second chance he was asking for.

"Yes, Abby, I see that," Adam replied, finally admitting to himself this was probably the end.

"Adam, thank you," Abby said.

He just stared at her. "For what?" He asked, confused.

"Thank you for finally telling me the truth. It was something I really needed to hear," Abby told him.

"But giving you the truth ended my chances with you," Adam told her, almost regretting it.

"I guess you might look at it that way," Abby said, nodding, and then continued, "But I don't. The thing is, if you had trusted me, you would have told me the truth on our wedding day and have let me decide how to handle it then. But you didn't trust me and didn't tell me then. And now I can't trust you. It's over, Adam," Abby told him softly.

Adam just nodded.

"I have something for you," Abby told him, motioning towards the box sitting on the kitchen table.

"What is it?" Adam asked.

"It's stuff I've been holding on to for over a year and I need to give it back. You'll also find the engagement ring and necklace and earring set you gave me."

"That's yours, Abby," He said sadly, looking down at his feet.

"Adam, I can't keep it. You need to take it back," Abby told him while she was shaking her head.

Adam looked at Abby and said, "So this is it?"

Abby just nodded, getting tears in her eyes, while Adam grabbed the box, and walked towards the door.

Clearing her tears, Abby ran ahead to the front door and opened it for Adam.

"Goodbye, Adam. I truly hope you find happiness soon and hope you find a person who will give it to you." She told him, being honest.

"For whatever its worth, I do love you and always will. Goodbye, Abby." Adam said, kissing her on the cheek one last time.

Adam walked out the door and out of her life.

Abby watched him go, getting fresh tears in her eyes. She knew without a doubt she had done the right thing.

As much as the truth had hurt, she needed it to move on.

She picked up the phone and dialed Max's number.

"Well, it's over." She told Max.

"I think you have it wrong," Max replied.

"Huh?" Abby asked him.

"It's only the beginning," He replied.

The End

Epilogue

New Beginnings

As Abby packed the last box into the moving truck, she looked around her yard for the last time. It was finally spring with the lilacs in full bloom and the house Max had designed had finally been finished just that week.

Abby thought about all that had happened in the last ten months as she looked down at her hand with a wedding ring on her finger. She smiled as she thought about the wedding two months before, thinking it was the happiest day of her life.

After sharing a very long and cold winter together, Max had surprised Abby with a trip to Napa Valley. They rented the same cottage as she had stayed in on her last trip.

No sooner had they gotten to the cottage and walked inside, Max couldn't wait any longer and he knelt down on one knee, pulling out a little box.

"Abby, I love you. I want to be with you forever. Will you marry me?" Max asked her.

She gasped in surprise when he opened the box. It was the most beautiful pear shaped diamond ring she had ever seen, and it was sparkling up at her.

"I love you too, Max. Yes, I'll marry you," She replied to him, kissing him.

He slid the platinum engagement ring on her finger and kept her hand in his.

He barely gave her a moment to digest what had just happened. "No pressure, Abby, but when and where?" Max asked her.

Abby laughed, and then said, "When? Where?" thinking she had barely just been asked. In all honestly she'd thought of it multiple times in the last several months about when and where.

"Yes. Have you thought about it?" He asked her, hopefully.

"Yes, Max, I have. I'd really like to have a small ceremony, just the two of us and our parents. And Colleen and Tom, of course," She said. "What do you want?"

"That's exactly what I was hoping you'd say. What about the when? Do you need a lot of time?" Max asked her.

"Time for what? To think? Not at all. I think the sooner the better," She replied, thinking he meant in a couple months.

"Okay, then what about here, now?" He asked, a little nervously. When he'd booked the trip, he planned to propose. Then he thought about the house that was almost finished and he couldn't think of moving into the house she helped build without her.

"Here? In Napa valley? Now?" She asked, already getting excited at the thought.

"Yes. What do you think?" He asked.

"I think...it's perfect! It would be so romantic to get married here! I think our parents and Colleen would be a little upset, but they'd get over it," She said.

"Not if they were here," Max replied.

"Here?" She asked.

"Yes. I'll book them a flight and they could be here by the weekend." He told her.

Abby gave him a huge smile and jumped into his arms. "Did you just plan this all on the spur of the moment?" She asked him.

"No, it was on the plane on the way here," He replied, smiling.

A few short days later, a very small, intimate wedding took place at the little cottage in Napa Valley, in the little backyard which overlooked some of the most beautiful countryside in America. Their parents were there, as well as Colleen and Tom, and they all watched as the couple exchanged vows and made it official. George and Junie beamed proudly while Abby parent's looked on with tears of joy.

♥ ♥ ♥

Abby looked up to see Max waiting patiently for her by the moving truck. She was happy to be moving in to the new house with Max, but sad to be leaving the house she'd owned for several years.

Looking over at Max, she was happy he had included her in all of the plans from the beginning, making it just as much her house as it was his.

He had insisted she be part of every decision about carpet, floors, countertops, lights and everything else that went into a house. The whole process was a great experience and she was glad he wanted to include her on every detail. He did that, she knew now, because he wanted her there to share it all with him.

She closed her front door for the last time, and then walked around the moving truck and hopped up inside.

"You all set?" He asked her.

"I am," She answered, smiling.

They drove away together towards the home they'd possibly live in for the rest of their lives. She thought it was funny that the first time she saw him move away was when he went away to college and she was devastated. This time was very different.

It only took fifteen minutes to get to their new home. They pulled up in the long cement driveway that had been poured the week before and he parked the moving truck.

She still couldn't believe what an incredible place he'd designed and had actually helped to build with his own two hands. He was very proud of it and she was very proud of him.

They got out of the truck and they met at the back.

Abby grabbed Max's hand as he was about to lift the truck gate and said "Wait. Let's go in and see the place before we start moving everything. Besides, the rest of the crew should be here shortly to help."

"Okay." He agreed happily. Anything to make his wife happy, he thought. He was secretly hoping he could talk her into having a baby soon. He didn't want to wait long!

They walked into the house, hand in hand. When they walked into the front door, he looked down at Abby and smiled.

"I want to show you something," Abby told him, grabbing his hand.

"Okay." He repeated.

She led him up the beautiful wooden staircase, towards the bedrooms on the second level.

Max started getting excited, thinking he was going to get lucky before anyone else got there to help them move.

He had no idea what was in store for him. As she led him past their bedroom he felt a twinge of disappointment until she stopped in front of one of the other bedrooms, one he secretly thought would be perfect for their first child.

"Ready?" She asked.

"For what?" He asked her, getting nervous.

"You'll see," She said, and then opened the door to the bedroom.

What he saw inside the bedroom shocked him. Somehow, without him knowing, she had come in and decorated the room during the week. He saw yellow walls, a box with a crib in the corner, a changing table, a dresser, and tons of stuffed animals around the room. On the ceiling there was a mobile with Winnie the Pooh, Tigger, Eeyore and other characters swinging gently in the breeze.

"Does this mean...?" Max asked Abby and then looked at her, hope gleaming in his eyes.

"Yes." She answered, getting tears in her own eyes when she saw how excited he was.

"When, how long?" He asked her.

"I'm about two months along. I just found out last week. I think maybe there was more than a wedding in Napa Valley, Max." She told him.

He picked her up and hugged her, twirling her around the room. He noticed the only thing not ready was the crib.

"What about the crib?" He asked her.

"Well, I thought the daddy would want to put that together." She told him.

"Yes, the daddy definitely wants to put it together." He answered. Max's chest puffed out proudly.

"I love you Max," Abby said.

"And I love you. This is the happiest day of my life. I'm not sure if anything could ever top this," He replied, and then gave her a very soft kiss.

As they heard the front door open and Colleen and Tom yell up the stairs that the moving crew was there, they took one more second to just look at each other and enjoy the moment.

Book Two – Second Look

Adam and Jennifer's Story

Over a year after Adam left his bride at the altar; he still couldn't forgive himself. For a long time he had blamed the person who he thought was responsible. Jennifer showed up on his doorstep, telling Adam he was a father on the day of his wedding. Adam made the snap decision to leave his bride-to-be, fly out to California and get to know his daughter, Amber. He had been furious with Jennifer when a DNA test proved Amber wasn't actually his, and he left after a huge fight with her. Several months later, when he had tried to call Jennifer to check on her and apologize for his behavior, her number had been disconnected, she had moved out of her apartment with no forwarding address, and he hadn't been able to find her since. In thinking back, he knew Jennifer had been absolutely devastated and he felt horrible about it. All he wanted was to get ahold of Jennifer and apologize for his horrible behavior.

Jennifer Sylvester had made mistakes. A lot of them. The worst one was ever letting Adam Jackson walk out of her life. She loved him so much she could barely breathe, and she'd completely messed things up for everyone, including her daughter. It was devastating to find out Adam was getting married, but that didn't compare to finding out Adam wasn't really Amber's father. She was shocked and confused, because she hadn't been with anyone else at that time, at least not that she could recall. But DNA tests don't lie, right? Adam had gone home to go win back his true love, and Jennifer had moved away with Amber, to start over in a new city, with a new phone number and a new life.

When Adam finally finds Jennifer and Amber, is it too late for a new beginning?

Author Biography

Connie Stephany lives in Zimmerman, Minnesota with her husband of 24 years. They have three children; Hannah (married to Ethan with one baby named Eleanor), Bobby, and Zoey. They have two fur babies, a dog, Millie & a cat they call Kitty.

Connie lost her full-time career in IT and is now disabled due to many health conditions including Ehlers-Danlos Syndrome, Mast Cell Activation Syndrome. She has too many things to list, but she knows there are many of us out there with EDS and MCAS.

Milton Keynes UK
Ingram Content Group UK Ltd.
UKHW011307210923
429112UK00004B/272